# Visible Human

## Flash Fiction by

## Tom Hazuka

BLUE LIGHT PRESS · 1ST WORLD PUBLISHING

SAN FRANCISCO · FAIRFIELD · DELHI

Winner, 2025 Blue Light Book Award

*Visible Human*

Copyright ©2025 by Tom Hazuka

1st World Library
PO Box 2211
Fairfield, IA 52556
www.1stworldpublishing.com

Blue Light Press
www.bluelightpress.com
bluelightpress@aol.com

Book & Cover Design
Melanie Gendron
melaniegendron999@gmail.com

Cover Art
*Angel of the Presence 5e*
by Melanie Gendron

Author Photo
Christine Perkins-Hazuka

First Edition

Library of Congress Cataloging-in-Publication Data

ISBN: 978-1-4218-3576-1

Dedicated to

the memory of Kevin Ryan

A fine writer, and even better father and friend

# Also by Tom Hazuka

**Novels**

*The Road to the Island*
*In the City of the Disappeared*

**Young Adult Novel**

*Last Chance for First*

**Memoir**

*If You Turn to Look Back*

**Nonfiction**

*A Method to March Madness: An Insider's Look at the Final Four*
(with C.J. Jones)

*A Summer That Can Change Your Life* (with C.J. Jones)

**Anthologies**

*Flash Fiction*, editor (with James Thomas and Denise Thomas)

*A Celestial Omnibus: Short Fiction on Faith*, editor (with J.P. Maney)

*Best American Flash Fiction of the 21st Century*,
editor (with Mark Budman)

*You Have Time for This: Contemporary Short-Short Stories*,
editor (with Mark Budman)

*Sudden Flash Youth*,
editor (with Christine Perkins-Hazuka and Mark Budman)

*Flash Fiction Funny*, editor

*Short on Sugar, High on Honey: 7-13 Word Love Stories*,
editor (with Mark Budman)

*Flash Nonfiction Funny*, editor (with Dinty W. Moore)

*Flash Nonfiction Food*, editor (with Kathryn Fitzpatrick)

*Operation Panic: Cold War Stories of the Atomic Bomb*,
editor (with Jimmy J. Pack)

# Acknowledgements

*Anthem Journal:* "One Hump or Two?" "Visible Human"

*BITE: An Anthology of* Cheek Teeth *Flash Fiction:* "Daddy's Here"

*Blink Ink:* "Coal Train Through Patagonia," "House by the Tracks," "Digestion"

*Brilliant Flash Fiction:* "Nowhere Station"

*Camroc Press Review:* "Pedalphiles"

*Connecticut Review (*reprinted in *BITE: An Anthology of* Cheek Teeth *Flash Fiction):* "That's All You Have to Do"

*Connotation Press:* "All Members Must Attend," "The Hypocritic Oath," "The Threat of Fate," "No Beauty"

*Drunken Boat:* "Sunflowers of Evil"

*Elsewhere:* "Gretchen Explains Her Life on Election Day Morning, 1980"

*Fast Forward Press:* "Scholastic Aptitude Test"

*Fictive Dream:* "Mile High Club," "I Didn't Shoot Jesse James," "Rice"

*50-Word Stories:* "Red, Red, Red"

*Five Points:* "Liver"

*Fixional:* "Bludgeonism," "Ghost Broccoli"

*Flash: The International Short-Short Story Magazine:* "The Richest Source of Nothing," "Saab Story"

*Flash Boulevard:* "Pretty Good American," "The Deal," "Sidecar"

*Flash Fiction Magazine:* "My Heart Is at Stake"

*Funny Bone: Flashing for Comic Relief:* "Merry Andrew"

*Inscape:* "The Downside of Anything"

*JMWW:* "Pirate Man"

*The Journal of Compressed Creative Arts:* "Animal Cruelty"

*Juked:* "Collecting Trollopes," Drinquility and the Red Carpet," "Just One Rule," "Tongue Lashing," "The End of the After"

*Miramichi Flash:* "Nowhere Station" (reprint)

*New Flash Fiction Review:* "Dive"

*New World Writing:* "I Used to Be a Pirate"

*100 Word Story:* "Lagniappe," "Off Peak," "Community," "Drive Fast, Take Chances"

*101 Words:* "A Single Thing"

*Pure Slush:* "People Are Idiot's," "Dry Dream," "K Pasa," "Deadwood"

*Quarterly West:* "Homeward Bound," "Mixture," "Utilitarianism"

*Santa Fe Literary Review:* "Just Walk Away"

*South Dakota Review:* "Field Trip," "Endangered Species," "Religious Holiday"

*Spelk:* "The Pie-Eyed Piper"

*The Quarterly:* "Vaporware"

*The Stray Branch*: "Sucker Mom"

*Vestal Review:* "Headless Angel"

# Contents

## Family Matters

## Nests and Other Things to Leave

## Working It

## Off the Road

## Pretty Good Americans

# Family Matters

# The Pie-Eyed Piper

King wrote lovely fiction no one would publish. "This is a beautifully written slice of life," editors would jot on rejection after rejection, "but there's no conflict, no *story*." Then, almost inevitably, "Please feel free to try us again."

King hated conflict, period, and couldn't fathom why anyone would go looking for it, whether in life or in literature. He read and enjoyed books, including most of the agreed-upon greats. What made his heart hurt with joy was not trouble, but sentences. Lying on his futon he would read his favorite ones aloud, savoring the delicious words, practically tasting them.

He didn't make a religion of geniuses unrecognized during their lifetimes, though he did make a shrine of sorts. A shelf in his basement studio apartment displayed a faded van Gogh self-portrait, a cracked-spine paperback of John Kennedy Toole's *A Confederacy of Dunces,* and a daguerreotype of Emily Dickinson in a heart-shaped frame. There was also a silver dog whistle on a loop of braided fishing line, though King had never owned a dog. His father's allergies to animal fur had meant no pets during King's childhood, and King understood why when he'd tried to share the studio with a kitten last week, and sneezed so frantically he had to give Emily away to a co-worker at the library.

When he told his parents the sad news about Emily, and revealed that he shared his father's allergy affliction, they exchanged a look of shocked conspiracy and burst out laughing.

His mother set down her mug of Nescafe. "Dad's not allergic to anything but hard work, Boo-Boo. That allergy story was his idea to keep you from begging for a pet."

"We should have got Academy Awards," his father said. "Talk about irony that *you're* allergic!"

She patted King's hand. "You don't have to thank us, dear. We're just good parents who sheltered you from reality."

That night after work, King started a story about a kitten that came frolicking to her master whenever he gently blew his slightly tarnished dog whistle. She curled up purring on his chest and dreamed of chasing a mouse should one ever climb high enough to invade her master's penthouse.

His working title was "The Pie-Eyed Piper," but that didn't matter because he knew it would never be published. Who wants to read a story where nothing happens?

# I Used to Be a Pirate

My future father-in-law squints at me from under a battered Red Sox cap. "Is it true that it's never too late to start an exercise program?"

"Sure," I say.

"OK, then I'll wait." Ken guffaws, breasts bouncing beneath his I BEAT ANOREXIA T-shirt.

I try to smile, hoping it doesn't look like a grimace. Ken is dangerously overweight, and Carol is worried about him. Close enough that I feel the heat on my neck, an enormous, unlucky pig slowly revolves on an electric spit. Horseshoes clank in the pair of pits across the yard.

"Cheers, buddy. Welcome to the family." Ken extends his beer and I raise mine to meet it; instead of a clink, our koozie-clad cans silently bump foam rubber.

Ken covers one eye with his beer. "Did you know I used to be a pirate?"

"No kidding."

"Oh, yeah. My favorite letter is 'RRRR.'"

I know I'm expected to laugh. I feel my lips curling in awkward directions.

"My theme song was 'Yo ho ho and a bottle of Tums.'"

I'm doing the math in my head, wondering how many times a year I'll have to deal with this guy. How could someone as cool as Carol possibly be his daughter?

I grasp at a straw the size of a javelin: maybe he's just testing me. Maybe he's checking to see if I love Carol enough to put up with this.

"Good one, Ken."

He leans a little too close. "Did you know I'm watching my weight? I'm watching it increase." He points to my beer. "Need another one?"

"No thanks, I'm good." I still have half a can of Bud Light.

Carol warned me that's what Ken would provide, so I brought a twelve-pack of Sam Adams and added them to the cooler. When I returned after my first beer, all but two were gone.

"Suit yourself." He claps me on the shoulder and stares into my eyes. "Carol's a very lucky girl, and so are you."

I wait for the chuckles because he called me a girl. Instead, his eyes stay locked on mine. "Promise me you'll take good care of my baby."

"Definitely. I promise."

"Who knows how long a fat bastard like me will be around, you know what I'm sayin'?"

"Ah, come on, you—"

"Yeah, I know, I'm in shape. Round is a shape."

He releases my shoulder. "I'm trusting you," he says, voice breaking a little.

I watch him trudge toward the nondescript house that's now part of my life. On the deck in a light blue sundress, Carol waves and blows me a kiss, then takes her dad's arm as they walk inside.

# That's All You Have to Do

Molly and her brother Pete were going fishing. She had never gone before. Usually Pete told her to get lost, because he was eleven and she was only eight, but Dad said Pete could use his fishing rod if he took her, and Molly would use Pete's. "Sweet," Pete said, because Dad's gear was a lot better than his. Besides, he told Molly as they walked down the road, "If you spaz and break my rod Dad will have to buy me a new one."

The pond was only fifteen minutes away. Molly was so excited she could barely stand it. She hoped people would see them and think she went with her brother to Porter's Pond all the time. She started to skip but forced herself to stop before Pete could turn around and make fun of her.

At the dam a short, scrawny man stood fishing with a long bamboo pole, no reel, line just tied at the end. His straggly gray hair jutted out from under a Ken's Kar Kare baseball cap that was so filthy Molly wasn't sure what color it used to be. They edged closer, Molly a step behind her brother.

The man turned his head and smiled at them. He had more wrinkles on his face than teeth in his mouth. Molly took a step back.

"Hi," Pete said.

The man tipped his cap with a hand that held a burning cigarette. Coughing, he pulled a small bluegill out of the water. With the cigarette dangling from his lips, he unhooked the fish and tossed it in a dirty yellow bucket. The pail was half full of water, and a bunch of bluegills.

He baited his hook with a new squirming worm. Molly saw parts of tattoos through the holes in his T-shirt. Without rinsing his hands in the lake, he put the cigarette back between his fingers.

"What're you going to do with them, mister?" Pete asked.

"What do you think, boy? Fry 'em up."

"You eat *bluegills*?"

"Ain't no meat sweeter. And the price is right."

"Our dad uses them for fertilizer--plants them in the dirt with corn seeds like the Indians did."

The man swung out his line. "Everything's got a purpose on God's green earth."

"Goodbye, mister." With one hand in his pocket, Pete waved with the other.

The man nodded, exhaling a cloud of smoke. "Don't do anything I wouldn't do," he said.

Molly wanted to say goodbye too, but no words came out. She followed her brother. Down the road Pete showed her the red and white plastic bobber he'd stolen.

"But he was *poor*," Molly said.

"He had a bunch and we only had one. Now you have one too. Or would you rather give it back?"

Molly had no answer. They cut into the woods and climbed over a stone wall. Pete rolled over a rotten log and found some fat worms. "Come on," he said. "I know the best place."

She followed him a few hundred feet through the trees to a quiet cove. Pete put the bobber on her line but said she had to bait her own hook. "If you're too much of a baby I'll never take you fishing again."

The worm was slimy in her hand. Molly dropped the slithery thing twice before she felt the sharp hook pop through its skin, and it wriggled like mad. She wasn't sure how to cast but didn't want to have to ask Pete.

Before she could try, though, he let out a whoop and started reeling. "Bluegill! Bigger than any *that* guy had."

The fish flopped at the end of his line. Grinning at Molly, Pete took a cherry bomb out of his pocket. He handed her a pack of matches.

"Light one," he said. "That's all you have to do."

He unhooked the fish. It gulped air, its eyes wide and staring. Pete popped the bomb in its mouth like a grape. He had to force it, but just a little. The waterproof wick stuck out like a cigarette.

"Come on, *light* it. Unless you don't want to go fishing anymore."

Molly's heart thumped against her ribs. "We're not supposed to play with matches."

Pete spat on a lily pad. "This isn't playing," he said.

Molly struck two match heads to shreds before the third one caught fire. Pete brought the bluegill to her trembling hand. The wick sizzled and he tenderly placed the fish in the water. Long seconds passed. Then a muffled explosion broke the surface ten feet offshore.

Pete laughed. "Cool, huh? I can't believe he got that far!"

"Cool," Molly said, her throat so tight she could barely talk.

Pete threw out another cast, halfway across the cove. He shook his head. "I can't believe that guy is low enough to eat bluegills."

Molly dropped the dead match in the water. A fish poked it twice before realizing it wasn't good to eat.

Molly turned away so Pete wouldn't see her wipe the tear off her cheek. Then she pressed the button on the Zebco 202 reel and carefully cast out the worm and the stained, stolen bobber.

"Pretty darn good for your first try, Moll," Pete said, and though her stomach felt full of worms his little sister couldn't help smiling.

# Daddy's Here

I'm supposed to pick up my son at three. I get there half an hour early.

"Daddy's here!" Jim calls through the screen door.

"I thought you said three," my ex-wife says.

"What? Am I late?"

Beth rolls her eyes. "Go someplace close," she says. "Get him home for supper, okay?"

"We'll have fish," Jim says. "I'll catch 'em."

"Actually, we'll throw them back if we get any. I know how much your Mom likes to clean fish."

Beth nods. "It's right up there with toothpicks under the fingernails. Give me a kiss."

I do, a quick one on the mouth. She's caught so off guard she blushes, something I've rarely seen. "Oh, you meant *Jim?*" I say, and feel the heat in my own cheeks.

"You're funny, Daddy," Jim says.

"Get out of here, both of you," Beth says, sounding scarily like my mother.

I put my son's gear next to mine in the back seat. We drive three miles to Porter's Pond and park on the side of the road. A short walk through the woods there's a shallow cove I know about, with a submerged stone wall thirty feet offshore. What *was* this place when the wall was on dry land, when someone had spent months creating it? Fish congregate around the wall, and Jim's in no danger of getting hung up. He's only six years old and probably can't cast that far anyway.

The ground is damp from the rain, even in the woods. We turn over a rotten log and a few rocks, and in five minutes have more than enough bait.

"Want me to put the worm on your hook?"

"I know how."

He doesn't, not really, but after a few tries and a lot of squirming the worm ends up skewered. It doesn't matter; sunfish will hit anything. I clip on a plastic bobber two feet from the hook. The first cast goes backward, and the second, and I have some untangling to do in the bushes. Finally, he gets a decent one out there, ten feet or so.

"Beautiful, Jimbo!" I say, and my boy tries to pretend he's not proud of himself.

The red and white bobber sits motionless on the skin of the pond. We watch it like campers around a fire, as if a secret waits inside. Suddenly it wiggles, just barely, so little at first that any kid's imagination could do better. But then it starts dancing. My son's eyes come alive.

"Now!" I say.

The fish hooks itself. I see Jim's clenched teeth as he reels. His cheap little pole bows hard toward the water, and for a weak moment I almost reach to help him. But I resist the impulse and leave him alone.

A bluegill flops in the air at the end of the line, twisting, fighting to throw the hook. Jim keeps cranking though the bobber is already jammed up against the rod tip. The drag screeches.

"You got him," I say. "Stop reeling." He does, watching the fish struggle. Amazement a pulse away from fear shines in his face.

"Do you want me to take him off the hook?"

He shakes his head.

"Do *you* want to?"

He swallows and doesn't answer.

"Grab him on the belly. He won't hurt you."

He reaches but the fish jumps and his hand shoots back. Again and again he tries but the bluegill has plenty of life left, plenty of fear to keep him thrashing.

"Let me do it for you."

My son won't look at me. He drops the pole and lays the fish on the shore where it bucks madly, coating itself with dirt, rubbing off its protective slime. Jim pins it to the ground with his sneaker. He squats and works. The hook is deep, too deep for me to see. When he finishes, he lifts his foot. The fish doesn't move.

My son squints at his bloody hook. I prepare to comfort him, to tell him these things happen boy but your Daddy's here, it'll be all right.

"Jerk ate my worm," he says, and reaches in the coffee can for another one.

# Liver

The night my father left us for the last time, my mother cooked liver for dinner. She probably knew he wasn't coming back, ever, but for me his empty chair wasn't unusual. I had never eaten liver before and spit out the one disgusting bite I took. My mother didn't even battle with me for refusing to eat, outside of saying how good for me the horrible stuff was, how it would make me grow up big and strong.

That was the one time during my childhood she let me have dessert despite not finishing what was on my plate.

# Sucker Mom

Everything's artisanal this, boutique that these days. But really, Slippery Slope Vodka? What was my son thinking? Sure, there's a snow-covered mountain on the label, tall as an Alp though we're in Connecticut, but still. I can't figure out if he's immune to connotation, or just going for cheap irony. Whatever, the overpriced stuff is selling decently and Curtis wants to expand capacity, add workers and increase advertising, maybe put out a variety flavored with some trendy fruit like acai or baobab—organic, of course.

All he needs to fulfill his dreams is a loan from his mother. His recovering alcoholic mother.

To his credit Curtis did try the bank first, but they turned him down because (speaking of his credit) he owes eighteen grand on his MasterCard, and already has mortgages on the business and his house.

"You have to spend money to make money, Mom," he said, sounding eerily like his father before he invested in that uranium plant currently eroding like a dinosaur skeleton in the Utah desert. "I'll pay you back with interest or give you a share of the company that will be worth a lot more."

Curtis wasn't all that indulged for an only child, though any spoiling usually started on Larry's end. "Go ask your mother," he'd say.

"Let me think about it," I told him.

The blue bottle of Slippery Slope sits on the coffee table where Curtis left it. ("Actually, Mom, it's azure, not blue. We did market research.") I haven't had a drink in so long—thirteen years this Thanksgiving—that Curtis probably doesn't think I'll even be tempted. He wants me to show it off to my friends, proud of my entrepreneur son, and maybe snag a few new customers.

I remember my days as a soccer mom, driving Curtis to practice and games. Of course people thought—at least I hoped they thought—that only coffee was in my Dunkin Donuts travel mug. More often than not, though, I was sipping gin gimlets instead of Colombian dark roast. I never left the house without a cache of Altoids in my purse and my car.

Then came the day I ran a red light on Route 15. Curtis and his friend Josh were playing video games in the back seat and had no clue what I'd done, even after the car I nearly broadsided blasted its horn.

Curtis looked up from his Game Boy. "What's that jerk's problem?"

I tried to respond but I couldn't breathe, couldn't swallow. If that car hadn't hesitated coming out of Middletown Road I might have killed someone. I might have killed all of us.

At the field I poured my gimlet down the Port-O-San hole, watching it splash into the gross blue (definitely not azure) goop. I haven't had a drink since.

It took me another four years to give up smoking, which I did the day we learned Larry had lung cancer. It was the least I could do considering the cruel joke that he was a non-smoker. I felt guilty about decades of subjecting him to secondhand smoke from my Winstons, though of course we couldn't know for sure what caused the tumors. I maybe killed my husband slowly, but for sure I nearly killed my son in a careless instant.

The Slippery Slope is just an easy reach away. I wonder if it has a screw cap or some trendy cork stopper.

Not long before the end, my husband said with a tight smile through the pain, "If you want God to laugh, make plans."

Only one way to find out.

Larry left me his teacher's pension and a few decent investments, better than the uranium mine anyway. I'm sixty-two so could start collecting Social Security. I was going to wait a few more years so the payment would be higher, but who knows, some drunk might run a red light and punch my ticket tomorrow.

We would always drink to celebrate, and toast to good fortune, to good times, to a smiling future with no fangs showing. I grip the neck of the azure bottle, missing my husband so much that my bones hurt. I realize I'm going to lend my son money I barely have, for a share of something that might fly high, but will probably crash and burn.

The screw cap opens with a crack like a snapping wishbone.

# Rice

Sarah has eaten rice probably a thousand times in her life, and rice was always just rice. So why did a casserole Peggy brought over four days after the funeral make her think of the time her mother made her kneel bare kneed on uncooked rice?

Sarah would have been six or seven, eight at most. She can't recall what crime she committed, but it must have been on Mom's list of mortal sins because she would usually just yell or give a quick slap on the ear. Sarah doesn't even have a sharp memory of what the rice felt like under her knees, just a certainty that from that moment on her mother could not be trusted. And Sarah never trusted her again.

She was against Sarah marrying Mark, of course. "No offense, blithe spirit, but men are scum and marriage is for suckers." Sarah didn't think her dad was scum, didn't blame him for divorcing her mother, and enjoyed spending time at his new house with his new wife. At the wedding, while other guests showered them with rice, her mother pelted them with it like a kid in a snowball fight. She hit the open bar hard at the reception. Gin and tonic in one hand, clinging to Mark's arm with the other, she grinned at Sarah as she pressed her chest against him. Sarah had never seen him look so uncomfortable.

"Just like you lovebirds have a year to write thank-you notes, I have a year to get you the perfect wedding present."

Their forty-ninth anniversary was last week, with Mark in hospice the day before he died. He was on so much morphine, Sarah doubts he knew what day it was.

Her mother's gift never arrived. Her father and Ruth gave them a bone china set she still uses.

Sarah thinks of the role rice has played in her life. A minor character, for sure, but some cameos were memorable. Like when she ate Rice-A-Roni at Cindy Grogan's house, and asked her mother later why they never had "the San Francisco treat."

Exhaling smoke from both nostrils, Mom stubbed out her Salem in a clamshell ashtray.

"Because it's poison, that's why. The salt will kill you."

She remembered rice casserole in the school cafeteria, lunch ladies scooping it from trays and plopping it onto plates like maggot ice cream. That's what the boys called it, anyway. Sarah thought it was tasty, though she would never have said so.

Mark once bought a twenty-pound sack of rice at India Mart, happy with "the economy of scale." But Sarah didn't cook rice all that often, and weevils infested the bag before it was half gone. How gross to think that eggs must already be on the grains, waiting to hatch if you don't eat them first.

"Gee, Mark," he said, "that certainly was a brilliant purchase." He smiled at Sarah. "False economy," she heard as he lugged the squirming bag to the trash can.

At both their sons' weddings no one threw rice, because people had learned that when birds eat rice it expands in their stomachs, possibly killing them. The only problem with that knowledge, scientists discovered, is that it's not true. Eating rice doesn't harm birds. Still, at their granddaughter's wedding the guests tossed birdseed. Mark said it looked like something that belonged on a bagel.

She misses him like crazy. She wonders when it will start to hurt less, if it ever will.

The thought of pain sends her to the pantry. Sarah knows it's melodramatic, knows it's ridiculous, but she takes two pinches of rice from a one-pound bag and places them on the kitchen floor. There are only a few grains in each group, not the bigger piles her mother had made. Sarah counts: six in one group, seven in the other. Thirteen has always been her lucky number. Mark's was seven, Mickey Mantle's baseball uniform number.

She smiles at memories of Mark playing softball. He was really good until he hurt his back and quit. He could have still played, carefully, but said that if he couldn't slide or dive for balls there was no sense playing at all. She used to love wearing his softball jerseys that were too big on her.

    The little constellations of rice suddenly look silly on the floor, meaningless specks waiting to be swept away. Sarah picks them up, drops them in the garbage and goes to search the back of her husband's T-shirt drawer.

# Nests and Other Things to Leave

# All Members Must Attend

John Owens rolls over for the fiftieth time tonight, stuffing the clammy sheet between his legs to buffer sweating skin. The single window in his studio apartment has no AC unit, just a ratty, ill-fitting screen. Sleep would be elusive in this heat under any circumstances, but Dennis and Delilah, the drug dealers who live above John on the fourth floor, are at it again. "At it" as in fighting, not having sex, though the latter coming from that apartment is nearly as noisy as the former, and often as long. John only knows their names because they get used a lot during both activities.

He opens a gluey eye to check the clock. 3:41 in the morning.

A nearby voice bellows like a wounded bison, "Yo, douchebags! PEOPLE ARE TRYING TO SLEEP!"

Weirdly, after a perfunctory "Eat me!" (from Delilah, not Dennis), the arguing stops dead. Of course, anyone who miraculously slept through the fighting was probably jolted awake by its even louder cure.

John has a gruesome thought: What if they think *he* is the one who yelled at them? He stretches his arms cruciform, trying to soothe his suddenly pounding heart. Dennis doesn't seem like the sense-of-humor type, except possibly if it involves inflicting pain. Listening hard for angry footsteps approaching his door, John whispers "om" over and over at the ceiling, which only increases his stress when he realizes he doesn't know if it's pronounced "ahm" or "ohm."

Maybe moving to the city after graduation wasn't the best plan after all. The prospect of being murdered in a case of mistaken vocal identity, or for any other reason, is not overly attractive. He prefers his heart to function unobtrusively, behind the scenes, not thump like a cheap speaker with the bass cranked to ten.

Less than four hours—if he survives—till John has to get up for another soul-deadening day at SpecTech. His dream job after college within two months has already curdled. He hates going to the office, which is even harder to admit to himself than it is to imagine telling his father that he's quitting. Craig Owens has never quit anything, especially telling anyone who'll listen that he has never quit anything.

John shifts to a modified fetal position. Unbidden, a sharp memory arrives of a handwritten sign he'd seen last fall, taped to a wall in the Humanities building:

PHILOSOPHY CLUB MEETING
ON FREE WILL
ALL MEMBERS MUST ATTEND!!!

No way. Are they serious? Glancing left and right, John snatched down the paper and hurried away, feeling like a shoplifter.

That night he and his roommate got stoned and laughed at the sign, now decorated with rings from their sweating beer cans.

"Evidently philosophers are impervious to irony," said Cosmic Dan, smoke seeping from his nostrils.

"Aren't *you* a philosopher, Cosmic?" John said.

Smiling, Dan packed another bowl. "Dude, I belong to no club that would have me as a member."

A siren wails somewhere, then recedes into the city. For the first time, John wonders if anyone missed that mandatory meeting because of him, because he grabbed that sign of his own free will.

Then something else occurs to him. What if somebody put that thing up as a joke, and *he* was the schmuck who didn't get the irony and believed it?

Overhead, the feral cries of make-up sex invade the neighborhood.

# Endangered Species

He drags himself into the apartment after another forever day at the office. Fortunately, serious money makes it all worthwhile. Anyway, it's not like he's going to do it forever. He's had this conversation with himself a hundred times, a thousand: make hay while the sun shines, pal, because who knows when that rain's coming. He loosens his tie, drops his briefcase on the couch. Goes to the kitchen for a beer. Wonders where the hell she is.

There's a note by the cutting board, on her Save the Manatees stationery. He gets the beer before picking it up, unfolding it. Out falls a check. "My half of the rent," he reads, "even though I'm leaving before the end of the month." Below that, in handwriting so much neater than her usual scrawl, is what he supposes has to be called a poem.

Thank You for Saying Goodbye

I saw through you
    almost from the first,
but I was horny and needed
    someone to write poetry to.

He has never known her to write a poem. Ever. He hated poetry in school, and he hates it more now. There was at least an excuse then, a teacher who forced it on you, a test you had to pass. He glares at the words. They don't even rhyme. And *he* wasn't the one to say goodbye. Ridiculous. Typical. Poetry—the word sounds like you're trying to spit out something that tastes bad. Something rotten. Feeling like he's been kicked in the gut, he takes a pen from his pocket and begins rhyming the first vicious words he hopes will help.

# Scholastic Aptitude Test

"If a baker's dozen is thirteen, what's eleven? A faker's dozen?" I smile across the table at my blind date, figuring that's the expected reward for her cleverness. She reacted to my comment about *Cheaper by the Dozen*, how insane it must be dealing with so many kids. But instead of smiling, she's on the verge of tears. I'm on the verge of deciding to throttle my sister Gail for setting me up with her fellow seventh grade teacher. Irene was "intriguing," said Gail's letters to me in Vietnam. Irene saw the world the way I did, "just off-kilter enough to make it interesting."

But off-kilter is the last thing I find interesting these days, so I stop pretending that my ex-wife is a blind date. That date happened over twenty years ago, the summer of the Watergate hearings, the summer I came home from the war. The Supreme Court had just decided Roe v. Wade. My date's wavy brown hair hung almost to her beaded belt. She wore turquoise earrings and an attitude foreign to any teacher I'd ever had, even in college. What my sister called "off-kilter," I called wonderful.

"If I made up the SAT, man," Irene said, "I'd ask relevant questions. Ones with answers like 'The Pope is to birth control as Nixon is to Vietnam.'"

We were halfway through our second Singapore Sling, and this comment seemed a revelation. This woman seemed like my answer. When we revealed that we both got 1350 on the SAT, it seemed like a sign.

Now, halfway through our glasses of mineral water, we are deciding like rational adults how often I should see my two children, who after all have a stepfather who loves them and has feelings too. I think of the fetuses, one aborted, one miscarried, who would have been our children instead, because never did we plan on more than two.

My ex-wife looks strange with hair as short as mine. She notices me noticing.

"I felt like I needed a change." She kind of fluffs it up in back. "What do you think?"

"I know what you mean."

"That doesn't answer the question."

There's a catch in her throat. I cough to try and clear mine.

"Unless you can eliminate some of the wrong answers," I say to the ceiling, "you're better off leaving it blank."

# Pirate Man

A cloister of dripping laundry is my landscape today. Nixon is President and I'm eight years old, hiding in the bower of Mom's breeze-billowed sheets, a pirate in a secluded Caribbean cove. I grip a fierce plastic cutlass in my teeth and dare the world to dare me to use it.

Somewhere in the distance my landlubber brother's bouncing basketball thumps like native drums. I'm scared, but not enough to shirk my duty. A man does what a man has to do. Especially a pirate man.

I bend low to peer through a porthole, alert for the enemy, but the bounding main is empty of frigate or caravel. I pull the cutlass from my mouth and wipe spit on my shorts as if it's some scurvy dog's blood, which it soon will be if I have my way.

My father, the noble Randy Lowe, is wasting away in a castle's dismal dungeon. "Wasting away" were the words I just heard my mother, Lady Bev Lowe, say to her friend Gwen over cigarettes and Sanka at our kitchen round table.

"Two or three months, that's all they give him." The Lady Bev wept, and I crept away unobserved to my ship.

My time is short, my task daunting: to free the noble Randy from his black-hearted captors. I need to plan my campaign. I need to be a strong, brave pirate man to rescue my Daddy.

With my faded Superman sheet I wipe the briny water dripping down my cheeks.

# Drinquility and the Red Carpet

Trying to achieve drinquility via Red Draws (beer and V8), Mehrtens thinks about Academy Award speeches written but never delivered. Where are those pieces of paper? Do the losers keep them? For that matter, where do women keep them even during the ceremony? Tuxedos have pockets—at least Mehrtens supposes they do.

Valerie always hogged the TV for the Oscars, so until tonight he always watched, bitching about how lame they were.

He remembers the Oscars last year, when out of nowhere Valerie said "drinquility" during the award for Best Makeup, and they laughed like two kids on summer vacation.

Reaching for the V8, Mehrtens has to admit he sort of misses that.

# Utilitarianism

I return home for the first time as an adult. My parents greet me traditionally, Mom worrying "that woman" isn't feeding me enough, Dad crushing my hand lest I forget which one of us survived the Tet Offensive. But an odor of arrested decay has replaced the smells of childhood. The house of my youth is decorated with death.

Stuffed creatures fill the rooms. Local varmints predominate—squirrels, chipmunks, some possums and porcupines, even a bullfrog—but Dad hangs my coat on an eight-point buck, and the TV blares from the belly of a rampant and silently roaring grizzly. We stand entranced, almost touching.

"I bet you could eat a horse," Mom says, and bustles to the kitchen.

"You know Jeremy Bentham, the philosopher?" Dad asks. "*He's* stuffed. Mom and I are going to London to see him."

My father has hardly left the state since Vietnam.

"Your favorite! Liverwurst on rye."

Mom puts the sandwich and a glass of milk on the dining room table. Then I see that the cat I grew up with is the centerpiece.

"You embalmed Kitten!"

"Embalming is for graveyards, son. Mom and I fixed Kitten to be with us forever."

I can't eat with a corpse staring at me. "Where did you get all these, these *dead* things?"

"My God, son," Mom says. "Open your eyes." A shadow nicks her face. "I thought you loved liverwurst."

"Your mother saw the ad in the magazine," Dad says, the two of them beaming as he puts his arm around her for the first time in my memory.

# Working It

# No Beauty

Watching in horror as my cubicle mate Dawson cleans his ear with a straightened paper clip, I remember Kayla Dowd singing as she undressed in front of a Michael Jackson poster in her bedroom. I have no idea why that memory returned. Sure, I hate my job, but I hate my job every day without Kayla's image showing up. I've seen Dawson risk a punctured eardrum with a paper clip before, and never thought of her. Possibly it has something to do with my thirty-fifth birthday tomorrow, or that the hospital should have called with my mother's test results by now.

Watching Kayla disrobe was neither an erotic nor a noble high point of my life. I did it while wedged in the crotch of a maple tree outside her second-story window. My friend Grimes, who had instigated this voyeurism and dared me to do it, sat on a lower limb hissing up to me for details but too chicken to climb any higher. We were twelve, hormone bombs barely primed. Kayla was in high school, a junior or some such impossibly advanced and mature age. She was no beauty, but Grimes claimed a few extra pounds just meant "more cushion for pushin'," and since he had two sisters and I had none, I semi-believed him.

Somehow, I don't think she was singing *to* Michael or *like* Michael; he just happened to be tacked on her wall, wearing a snappy fedora and a single glittery glove—which was soon more than *she* was wearing. With the window shut I couldn't tell if she was singing along with something or going it a cappella.

"Whaddya see, Burton? Whaddya see?"

I saw that her eyes were closed as her full, lovely hips swayed to a rhythm I couldn't hear, and in the first truly sad moment of my life I rested my chin against a branch's bark and with eyes wide open realized that maybe I never would.

"Nothing," I whispered down. "I don't see anything."

Dawson pauses in his probing, squints at me. "Don't give me that superior look, Burton. My ear itches—what do you want from me?"

# Community

Connie huddles near the doorway with the other seven smokers from the office, trying to avoid a slanting downpour, enduring dirty looks from the pure-lunged majority who pass through the cancer cloud they're creating. Marge Cochran from Accounting even fakes a hacking cough, that sanctimonious bitch.

Connie leans her back against the NO SMOKING WITHIN 25 FEET sign, blocking the circled cigarette with a red slash through it. She wonders which is harder, quitting smoking or finding a single thing she has in common with these people besides an addiction.

Suddenly everyone starts laughing at something, so Connie laughs too.

# Lagniappe

McGrath stands up from the ripped red Naugahyde couch to stretch his back. He's been at Autofix nearly three hours, waiting for a part so precious that apparently no warehouse dares to stock it. He can't drink any more bitter, sludgy coffee, and feels guilty for punching the planet in the balls by using a Styrofoam cup. He brought a book, but blaring TV game shows make reading impossible.

"Sir, if it's any consolation, there's a set labor charge for the job, no matter how long it takes."

"Gee, I feel better already."

And somehow, sort of, he actually did.

# Just Walk Away

I'm making a deposit at the bank, a half-decent check from a house painting job, paid under the table. Thinking again about what Susie said last night, I look past the teller to the drive-up window, where a red-faced, beefy bastard in a tight T-shirt and a Hummer ignores the other teller's thanks and advice to have a nice day. He drives off, eyes on his phone, texting with one hand. Through the space vacated by his obscene vehicle I notice the ATM in the outer lane, its front panel raised like the hood of a broken-down car.

Suddenly I have a reason to do more than just get through this day. Come on, come on, hurry up with that receipt. How often do you have a shot to see the guts of an ATM? For me, exactly zero times in thirty-six years on this planet.

The teller slaps down the slip of paper. "Have a nice—"

"You too," I say, already heading for the door.

I stride outside and around the corner, sure that with my luck, the machine's face will be snapped shut again. I stop, relieved to find the panel still open like an invitation. There's also something I couldn't see from inside the bank: a red Dunbar armored truck blocking access to the ATM. But that's only for cars. I can walk right up.

Still, something about those trucks is intimidating, shadows of Panzers blitzing across Poland. A tall guard in a crisp uniform finishes sliding a tray into the ATM. If there's such a thing as a noncommittal glare, that's what he gives me. I almost say the hell with it, but instead I step closer because we live in a free country, right?

"First time I've had a chance to look inside one of these things," I say pleasantly, as if I'm commenting on the weather.

The guy glares at me. "Just walk away."

What was I expecting to see—thick stacks of Benjamins? Instead, the money machine is about as interesting as the bowels of a printer. The tray he installed might as well be a toner cartridge.

"I'm not going to steal anything."

"I didn't say you were. Now walk away."

"Fine. Excuse me for having a little curiosity."

He shakes his head without looking at me. "You know what *that* did to the cat."

I feel my face twist as I roll my eyes. Seriously, dude? Seriously?

But those words don't leave my head, never make it to my mouth. Walking to my car I can't recall if he had a gun on his hip, but I'm not going to give that prick the satisfaction of seeing me turn around.

I hate my hand for trembling as I unlock my Grand Prix. Maybe Susie was right, maybe that *is* my problem—I just let the goddamn world happen to me. I might even tell her so if she ever answers my messages.

Sitting in the driver's seat, I think about that year I played Little League. I was small, skinny and scared of the ball, and only joined because my father pressured me. The coach would put me in for two innings a game, which I spent in right field praying no ball would come my way. The rare times I got up to bat I'd crouch low, creating a strike zone the size of a bull's-eye. "A walk's as good as a hit!" I'd hear through my helmet, yelled by my teammates, my coach, eventually even by my father. And I usually *would* walk. Everyone knew swinging was my worst option.

The Dunbar truck lumbers by like it runs the world. I expect some attitude from Mr. Armed Guard, protector of rich men's gold from no threat whatsoever, but the son of a bitch drives away like I'm not even here.

# The Deal

The waitress brings two beers and Meskill pays with a twenty peeled from his shrinking roll of cash. He can't risk his credit card being declined in front of a prospective buyer. He clinks old man Savage's glass and continues their conversation about baseball. "You're right," he says. "Gardner's got wheels. He hit a bases-loaded triple last night."

Savage squints in the shade under the Corona umbrella. "How many runs scored?"

Meskill takes a long pull from his pint and smiles the foam off his lips. He's starting to get a feeling that this will be a fruitful negotiation.

# I Didn't Shoot Jesse James

As names go, I could do a lot worse than Robert Ford. I'm not Adolf Hitler, for example, or Ted Bundy. Most people don't know jack about history anyway, so have no clue that Robert Ford shot unarmed Jesse James in 1882. Jesse stood on a chair to straighten a picture, and Bob pumped hot lead into the back of his head.

For the record, I probably would not have done that. I don't even own guns. Well, I used to; now I have only one, a .45 pistol I take to the shooting range every other blue moon.

My old friends call me Bobby; my new one calls me Bob. My mother calls me Robert when she's pissed at me, which happens somewhat less often these days. My father was also Robert Ford, and if he continues to walk this earth I assume he still is. I last saw him at Christmas when I was seven, twenty-three years ago. For my birthday that June he took me to the range, and nearly died laughing at how scared I was of the noise, trembling like a poodle on the Fourth of July. It was the first time he called me a pussy, and the last time he said it with a smile.

My mother always called him Bob no matter how ticked off she was at him. To me she calls him "your father." To her friends, though, he's often "that bastard," likely echoing Frank James' name for the Judas who murdered his brother. On the off chance you care, Bob Ford was gunned down ten years later in a saloon he owned. He was thirty.

I'm thirty. Something should have happened in my life by now. I should have a girlfriend, or a wife, maybe even a kid or two. I should have moved on from my job at the lumberyard, where I'd planned to work the summer after high school while I figured out what my real life would be. I did grunt work at first, then drove a forklift for ten years until the owner made me a dispatcher, which pays better but the stress is giving me an ulcer. I started smoking again, and a pack of Marlboros a day burns up an unhealthy chunk of my raise.

The truth is I don't know jack about history, either. I know Bob Ford for the same reason I'd know Watergate if my name was Richard Nixon. How could you not be curious? Anyway, it's better than being named Michael Jordan or Tom Brady, where people smirk at you for not being the real one.

The other night I saw *The Assassination of Jesse James by the Coward Robert Ford* on TV. Casey Affleck played Bob. He was good, I guess, but sometimes I watch actors and think I could do that, or better. In a way, movies are easier than life because someone writes your lines for you. The hardest part is the audition.

Maybe I *am* a coward. Twelve years at Bascom Lumber are eleven too many, but a few guys have been there twenty or more and Manuel Lazardo has over thirty. Manny still smiles when they rib him for pronouncing "you" like "Jew," but he has a little limp now and sometimes groans when he stands up. He'll tell you he's just grateful to have a job after coming to this country with nothing. His wife cleans rooms at the Ramada, and they put four sons through college. I don't know what their kids do, but they damn sure don't work in a lumberyard.

I hear the community college takes anyone with a pulse. I could try that. I read and write halfway decent and could go at night. Maybe I'd meet a woman there, someone new, not the usual barflies at the Dew Drop Inn. I could sign up for one course, I don't know what, something interesting, something a smart, good-looking woman not prejudiced against lumberyard workers might take.

But I'm beat and frazzled after work—how could I even pay attention? Maybe she'll think I'm a dumbass. Maybe I *am* a dumbass, but I don't have to be the coward Robert Ford. I'm at least going to check the school catalogue, see if something looks good.

My brain might be shot, but it's all I've got.

# The Richest Source of Nothing

"What's worse," she asks, "being normal or being average?" She has lipstick on her teeth and a dandelion tattoo disappearing into her cleavage.

"Normal," I say. For me, "normal" and "average" represent unattainable heights.

I need to fix the sickness.

She sucks through her swizzle straw, slurping the dregs beneath melting ice cubes. She hopes I'll buy her a drink, but my wallet contains only three damp dollars.

"'Normal' is the richest source of nothing on the planet, pal. You can take that to the bank."

Thinking about withdrawals and interest, I don't flinch when her hand grips my thigh.

# Deadwood

On the ides of March 2020, Will Harrington read an essay from his best student about the chaos that ensued when the university abruptly closed the dorms during Covid-19, stronger people shoving weaker ones aside in a frenzied rush to the exits. Becky was an RA and saw the whole sorry spectacle.

Her essay, "Oh, the Humanity!", came via email because Covid had forced classes online and students couldn't distribute paper copies of their workshop submissions. Class that day started ten minutes late when the student who had volunteered to initiate the Zoom session didn't send the link till then. Harrington knew he should learn to do it himself, but Covid had enlarged his already pronounced Luddite streak, and he just didn't feel up to it. He could stumble through seven more weeks till the semester ended.

At first, fifteen faces were on Will's screen, but gradually several were replaced by black boxes with the student's name in them. They had turned off their cameras, disappeared for one reason or another. Will considered calling them out, then decided to just mark them absent if they didn't return.

During workshops Will always had the author read a section from their piece. Becky chose her final paragraph, which ended, "Peel away a thin layer of civilization like sunburned skin, and we're all just animals out for ourselves."

No one spoke. Will cleared his throat.

"*All* of us? *You* stayed and did your job."

Becky smiled. "Maybe because I'm small and knew I'd get trampled if I ran."

"I thought the author couldn't talk," Xander said, annoyingly but not inaccurately, because one of Will's workshop rules was that the writer had to listen silently till the discussion ended.

"*Mea culpa*," Will said.

"Huh?"

"It means 'my bad.'"

"Why didn't you just say that?"

Will couldn't resist. "Because I'm a pretentious snob who likes to show off the few Latin words I know."

"Oh, OK."

"That sunburn image is gross," said Phil Clark, the worst writer in the class.

Will was ambivalent about the image, but it irked him that people like Phil would home in on one weak point rather than celebrate the excellence of almost everything else.

"I think it works," Wendy said, "because the people *act* gross."

"I like it," Heather said. "I have pale skin so I can relate."

"And Black people can't?" Phil said.

The one Black student in the class looked down and shook his head.

"I didn't mean that," Heather said, pale skin blushing.

"Yes, but—"

Harrington had to interrupt, for the sake of the workshop and his sanity. "This tangent is not helping Becky much."

Another face on his screen disappeared, replaced by a black box.

Suddenly, Harrington wondered what he was doing. Not just running a class on Zoom, but in general. Forced to teach on a screen, he had devolved overnight from an A- professor, maybe an A on his best days, to a C+ one. He knew he'd improve with practice, but he didn't want to put in the time, not at this point.

He was 66 years old. The semester was half over. His life was far more than half over.

"Can I talk now?" Becky asked.

"Sure."

She spoke cogently and intelligently. It was a pleasure to listen to her. For a naïve moment he assumed everyone felt the same way.

Then a black box replaced Phil Clark's face.

Zoom had allowed an untalented dimwit to ignore talented intelligence, just like that. In a classroom, Phil would have had to take a bathroom break to leave while someone was talking, which rarely happened. Online, people evidently felt it was OK to be rude, or that somehow leaving *wasn't* rude, which was just as bad.

After class Harrington stared at his laptop. Thirty years peeled away as he remembered some longtime professors during his first years here, burned out on teaching and cynical about students, hanging on just to increase their pensions. "Deadwood," people mockingly called them. Harrington joked with other junior faculty about aspiring to achieve deadwood status one day, a day impossibly far in the future.

This epidemic might last for years. Classes would undoubtedly still be online in the fall, and probably for the whole year--or longer. Harrington felt himself shriveling into deadwood at the thought of joining those laughingstock professors, hanging on past their sell-by dates.

Will marked Phil Clark absent then sat back and closed his watery eyes, at peace with his decision.

# Off the Road

# Headless Angel

Peggy was three months pregnant when she and Evan went to France on their honeymoon. The trip represented their promise not to let the baby change who they were, not to forget that there was so much world, all around, waiting.

Then, in Normandy, strolling down to the beach for lunch, they saw a woman jump from a fourth-floor window and die on the sidewalk, right across the street. It was horrible, a shock out of nowhere on a gorgeous sunny day. People ran to the rag-doll body, yelling for a doctor, yelling for the police. But it was hopeless. Peggy trembled against him in a way she never had before; Evan knew she was remembering her younger sister who had killed herself. Hugging each other hard, they walked to the shore. Young men in tiny bathing suits played volleyball on the sand, oblivious to what had happened two hundred feet away.

"It'll be all right," Evan said finally. He put the untouched baguette and Brie in his backpack, though he was very hungry. He squinted against the glare off the Atlantic. The water was cold here, all year round.

"Right," Peggy said.

The next day they drove the abbey road along the Seine. The river flowed slow and perfect in the morning mist. They stopped at the Abbaye de Jumièges and paid to enter the magnificent ruin, roofless walls and white stone spires reaching for the sky.

Peggy disappeared.

Evan found her in a courtyard staring at a decapitated marble angel, its childlike hands palm-to-palm in prayer, the front of its bare feet broken off and worn as smooth as a windowsill polished by generations of elbows.

Peggy touched the angel's wings.

"Vacation's almost over, lover," she whispered. "Soon we have to fly home."

Their fingers intertwined on the cold, hard stone.

# Nowhere Station

I was alone in a second-class car on a train out of Madrid, bound for Barcelona. Yesterday I'd spent twenty minutes standing in front of Picasso's *Guernica*, which was black and white like old war photographs and far larger than I expected. I was twenty years old. No painting could make me cry back then, at least on the outside. It was springtime in Spain. Franco had died last fall after 36 years as dictator, which meant little to me till I saw *Guernica*. I couldn't stop thinking about the painting.

The train stopped at some nowhere station. A small, gaunt man around sixty hesitated at the door of the compartment, then sat across from me by the window. I smiled and he smiled back.

There was a five-day beard on his sunken cheeks. He took a pack of Fortuna cigarettes from his shirt pocket and held it out to me.

"*No, gracias.*" That was about the extent of my Spanish, along with "*Buenos días*" and "*Una cerveza, por favor.*"

He shrugged and lit one for himself. He blew out foul-smelling smoke and made what seemed to be a friendly remark.

I knew one more thing in Spanish. "*No hablo español,*" I said apologetically.

He nodded. Easy math told me he was around twenty years old on April 26, 1937, the day Guernica was bombed. I wanted to ask—oh so carefully—about his life, what it was like to be twenty during a civil war rather than a college student traveling from across the ocean. I wondered if he had fought, and for which side. I wondered if he'd been to Guernica.

For many miles he smoked and I looked out the window, until without a word he touched my knee and left my life at another nowhere station.

# Coal Train Through Patagonia

We bummed a ride from Chile on a coal train bound for Rio Gallegos, Argentina, slow-clattering ten hours in the caboose, snaking through endless, glorious nothing, smoking cigarettes we got God knows where, because neither of us smokes.

Ah, Woody Guthrie, the songs we would have made if we only had our guitars.

# House by the Tracks

Forehead jostling on the train window glass, I remember Rachel's kiss goodbye and wonder if I'll ever see her again. We rumble past a crumbling farmhouse. Someone used to live there, I think; someone built that sunken roof and rotting porch.

The train clatters and shrieks and picks up speed.

# Homeward Bound

Thanksgiving, 1970, changing planes at a Midwestern airport. I wasn't feeling thankful, not even for my sky-high draft lottery number. I felt more guilty than good about luck shielding me from decisions I'd never wish on anybody: Canada, prison, Vietnam.

A soldier in a wheelchair was smoking Luckies like his life depended on it. He had a newspaper on his lap but wasn't reading it; I saw ashes on the headlines. After a while two soldiers sat in front of me, discussing the football game. One hoped the storm would hold off because he hated goddamn turbulence.

A guy and a girl my age—college—came up to the wheelchair. "Vietnam?" he asked.

The soldier nodded.

"Good," she said. "Paralyzed, babyburner? Still got your manhood?"

"Yeah," he said, too quick, so quick it made you wonder.

The bigger soldier jumped up, but the skinny one shoved him aside. He dropped the guy with one punch, then smacked the girl twice in the face.

A Black security guard my father's age ran over. "Did you *see* that?" the girl shrieked.

"I saw it." He yanked the guy to his feet. "Now *get* out of here."

His voice was so venomous they fled without speaking. The wheelchair soldier was shaking, pretending to read the paper. The other two sat down again, careful, like they weren't sure the seats fit any more.

"Sorry, man," said the skinny one, his voice full of holes. "I was afraid you couldn't do it."

I remembered going to Niagara Falls as a kid, the disappointment of crossing into Canada and not feeling any different on foreign soil. It was like the world was just all one place.

We took off late in the snowstorm.

# Mile High Club

Halfway back from Hawaii, most passengers on the red-eye are asleep. Despite popping two Benadryls, Hunter doubts he'll be able to join them. He glances at his wife, who has the gift of crashing anywhere. Wrong verb on an airplane, he realizes.

Katie is staring at him. Hand stroking high up his thigh, she whispers warm in his ear.

"Bathroom on the other side is open. Mile High Club meeting in thirty seconds."

Hunter grins at the joke, but her eyes are dead serious. With a curt nod, like a soldier heading off on a mission, she gets up and strides toward the rear of the plane.

It's a great sign, right? Sex in the first two days on Kauai was followed by none in the last three, when Katie seemed a trifle cool toward him. Still herself, but definitely a link or two more distant in the chain that binds them.

Hunter unbuckles his seatbelt, armpits suddenly swampy. He sometimes kids Katie about his membership in the Mile High Club, which he joined courtesy of an ex-girlfriend who specialized in that sort of thing. Meanwhile Katie is still on the club's waiting list, where he assumed she wanted to stay.

He sidles up the aisle. Two flight attendants perch on fold-down seats, lost in a fashion magazine and a paperback. He taps the door. It accordions open and he pushes in. He shoves the door shut, slides the bolt.

"The meeting will come to order," she says, reaching for his zipper. They wriggle each other's pants below their knees. In such cramped quarters there's only one real alternative.

"Bow wow," she says, and leans over the toilet with her hands on the wall.

Hunter tries to keep his jeans taut against his calves so they don't drop to the nasty floor. He's half an inch into Katie's initiation when the plane lurches down, then thrashes side to side. Hunter is flung away from her. Stuff rattles and bangs in the galley on the other side of the wall. Someone screams.

"This is Captain Collins. We've encountered some rough air. Return to your seats immediately and fasten your belts."

The plane is bouncing like the sky is full of potholes. Hunter detests turbulence, but trying to pull up his pants while holding the sink with one hand leaves him little time to be afraid.

Knuckles rap at the door. "Folks, return to your seats!"

Their eyes connect. *Folks?*

"Oh Jesus," Katie says.

Hunter gulps the knot in his throat. The plane bucks him into the door, and Katie into him.

Like drunks after last call they stumble into the aisle, clutching each other despite the embarrassment. A wrinkled harridan glares at them like Torquemada. They totter past the belted-in flight attendants. "Hurry, folks!" one orders, lips curling in a righteous, snotty-sweet smile Hunter recalls from his Bible Belt childhood.

They tip into their seats. Hunter's heart is thumping in his pulse points. He squeezes Katie's hand. Why? To reassure himself? She *enjoys* turbulence, thinks it's fun, like rocking a ski lift chair over jagged boulders a hundred feet below.

"So," she says softly, "how's it feel to get slut-shamed?"

"What? I mean…"

"Feels like the whole plane's looking at us, doesn't it?"

It wasn't my idea, he thinks. "Kind of."

Katie leans in close, like when she invited him to the bathroom. How long ago was that, five minutes? Less?

"Did you get it in?"

"You couldn't tell?" Hunter tries to sound aggrieved, but in the jerking aircraft all he sounds is scared.

"I maybe felt something." Katie peers past him to the bruise-colored clouds in the sunrise. Hunter can smell her shampoo—lemon, maybe, or some kind of flower.

"Any penetration," she says, "however slight, is sufficient to complete the offense."

51

"What are you talking about?"

"It's the army's definition of rape."

"How do you know that?"

"I picked it up somewhere, like an STD."

The plane shudders. Hunter grits his teeth and squeezes his eyes tight. He realizes this is a strange and memorable moment in his life, yet minutes ago he wouldn't have expected any of it.

Katie grips his wrist. "The point is that it counts. I'm in the club."

He considers quoting Groucho Marx about not wanting to belong to any club that would have him as a member. The bumps have leveled out, but he knows that could change in a second.

"Of course you are, baby," he says. "Of course you are."

# Till Sex Do Us Part

# The Threat of Fate

A biology professor in college once told our class, "Heredity is not fate; it is the threat of fate." I don't recall his name—this was fifteen years ago, maybe more—but I remember I disliked the guy until he said that. Somehow after I heard those words, his nerdy demeanor and inept attempts to disguise his stares at my chest didn't bother me anymore. He might have been a creep, but I knew he had given me something I wouldn't forget.

Jason insists he's not leaving because of my cancer, as if that somehow makes him honorable. He doesn't want me to think he's a coward for abandoning a sick woman, wants me to know he's treating me not *like* a sick woman, but like any woman he doesn't love anymore.

No, Jen, he might as well say flat-out, it's not breast cancer—it's you.

Angelina Jolie had hers removed in a preemptive strike and made the cover of *Time*: a profile photo in black and white, her arms crossed beneath the breasts whose days are numbered. She's wearing a dark sweater, though I bet *Time* was tempted to use a shot in her bosom-bulging *Lara Croft Tomb Raider* tank top. That probably would have sold more magazines, especially after the outcry over the crass exploitation. Considering the species we belong to, *Time*'s decision on the photo would have been bigger news than Jolie's decision to have the operation.

For me it's no decision. Life made it for me. I wonder what I'll look like when they're gone. Unlike Angelina, I have nowhere near enough money for reconstructive surgery. Facebook banned post-mastectomy photos, then allowed them again after thousands of people complained. Breast cancer survivors said the images empowered them. I have no reason to doubt those women or their motivation, but I'm far more frightened than I am curious, and there's no way I want to see those pictures.

Maybe it will be different once I can contribute my own.

Is it strange that I've started wondering what a baby's mouth feels like, using these glands for their anatomical purpose? I've never wanted to have children, but now I keep imagining holding a tiny infant close, Madonna-like, almost scared at her toothless urgency as I feed her with my body.

I'm not sure why it's always a girl. Maybe because to this point only male mouths have sucked these nipples. Milk-less male mouths, hungry, but not for food.

So…my time with Jason is over, three decent years down the toilet. He didn't leave me much, but like that biology prof—Carson, that's right, the guy's name was Carson!—he contributed one good line to my life, the motto we used whenever we caught ourselves bitching over trifles when things could be so much worse:

Suck it up, crybaby.

# My Heart Is at Stake

Call me Dracula. People say I'm a sick man, and though their condemnations pierce my heart, the claim is true. I *am* a sick man…a lovesick man. An undead lovesick man, to be sure, but those in love know not to split hairs.

I met Lotte Sanger at Transylvania Stadium. I was a relief pitcher for the Carpathian Wolves (who fortunately only play night games). My control could be erratic, and a wag sportswriter for the local rag dubbed me "Full Count" Dracula. I gently confronted him for hurting my feelings. "Bite me, Vlad," he said, and that midnight I granted him his wish.

Lotte sold beer at Wolves games and would periodically bring frothy cups to fortify the team. (Absurdly strict league rule: only one liter per player, with another half-liter for extra innings.) Our eyes met across a crowded dugout, and I was smitten. Lotte was as well, or so she later claimed, though lovers can be so competitive, vying to outdo each other as the most hopelessly *inamorato*, the one most like Saint Sebastian porcupined with Cupid's arrows.

Our first date was at Impaler's Steak House, my go-to joint where everyone knows my name. I got prime rib well-done so not to be distracted, but Lotte ordered a sirloin bloody rare. "Still mooing," she said with a smile, displaying adorable canines. We had Bloody Marys and a heavenly bottle of Hungarian Bull's Blood wine, then necked in the parking lot before repairing to my lair for postprandial low jinx under a cape in my coffin.

"Kinky," she said. "I'm impressed."

Henceforth, Lotte was my Muse of the Mound. My fastball picked up speed, my slider had more bite, and I was painting the corners, hardly walking anyone. I became the Wolves' closer and saved thirteen straight games without surrendering a run. Bats flapped helplessly against my stinging deliveries. My teammates razzed me when I came to the park with a hickey on my throat, but no one argued with the results.

"Steroids! 'Roid Boy!" taunted fans during road games, but I was only juiced on Lotte. I loved to mow down batters and suck the life out of a crowd in Suceava or Turda, leaving them drained and defeated. After every home game I hung upside-down in gravity boots and read *Batman* comics, keeping my spine limber to counteract the opposing hitters' lumber. Then Lotte and I would adjourn to my man cave to, as she liked to put it, "turn a double play."

"Think you can handle my high hard one?" I bantered once during the walk. Clouds scudded across a glowing gibbous moon.

Lotte licked her lips. "Anything but a dribbler back to the mound," she said. I've never met anyone who could scoff so lasciviously.

The season wore on, and wore down. A nip of Transylvanian autumn titillated the air as the playoffs started, the Wolves in first place with home field advantage throughout the postseason. Are you expecting tales of last-inning heroics, walk-off home runs and me closing games like a coffin lid? The reality was more mundane, and more dominant. We swept both rounds of the playoffs, and took turns hoisting the championship Strigoi Trophy. That night Lotte's kisses tasted of the Romanian sparkling wine we'd sprayed around the locker room like cats marking territory. It was the happiest I'd been in at least four hundred years.

The season ended, and so did my dream. For Lotte I was a summer fling, a toothsome diversion before she followed the sun far across the forest, to graduate school in America. She broke the mordant news as we strolled the shore of Lacu Mare, forever Lachrymose Lake to me now.

"You kept this a *secret*? Not a word all season?"

"At first it was just fun. And then…"—she stared at the stars—"and then I couldn't bear to spoil anything."

Sex under the night sky was as mournful as it was exhilarating. My fangs ached to enter Lotte's flesh, to make her mine forever. Her pale throat in the moonlight beckoned me like no temptation ever before, but in the name of love I forbore.

In the eternal, god-damned name of love, I forbore.

# Gretchen Explains Her Life on Election Day Morning, 1980

I'm Gretchen, which is a blessing and a hearse, like the battered black one my brother Bobby installed a turntable in back in '65, convinced he was a genius and soon to be rich when the idea caught on. But a bumpy road beat up the Beatles and scratched his plan.

I'm the only thing holding my parents together. At least that's what each tells me privately. "I'm not your adhesive!" I scream behind my eyes, sounding like a therapist in a movie that shouldn't have been made. No one hears. Bobby's no help. He turned to scope a girl riding a ten-speed down a mountain, smashed through guardrails and flipped his hearse over a cliff. That's her story, anyway, swears to God, and He and she were the only witnesses. Stack the Bibles, Beethoven, and turn a deaf ear.

They outlawed the head-slap in the NFL, that smack upside the helmet that turns your ear into a frozen sting, bad as a shot to the nose when blood and tears and snot mix like a drink on your lips, salty as a margarita. Deacon Jones told the TV camera it made a man—"or a woman"—blink, and that instant was all he needed to hammer the quarterback.

Adam grins, despite his hangover. He swallows the three aspirins I bring him. "I never mean to, baby," he says. "It just happens. You know I love you."

I go in to make breakfast. "Over easy," he calls from the living room. "Please." I hear the sports section rustle. I hear *Good Morning America.*

"Sunny side down, honey," he says. "And don't you dare break the yolk."

# Off Peak

The morning after Amy returned from her high school reunion halfway across the country, she introduced Cliff to a sex position he not only had never tried before, he'd never even imagined it. Despite its wonders he couldn't decide if the surprise was pleasant or not, because to his knowledge Amy was not the type to consult manuals. Maybe he should have caved in and gone to the reunion like she wanted. Maybe he shouldn't have insisted quite so vehemently that she'd have more fun without him. In the end, he had to admit she found a pretty reasonable flight.

# One Hump or Two?

"She speaks fluent Too Much," my new girlfriend Erin says about my old girlfriend Amy, which is weird because Erin is in the process of introducing me to a sexual position called The Limber Camel, and Amy is the only person I've heard use that line before. As I'm contorted in quest of kundalini ecstasy, I ponder whether these two women share some history, though for all I know it's the popular culture buzz phrase of the year. Neither word in "popular culture" applies much to me, after all.

With a pang I wonder what Amy is doing right now.

# Saab Story

I hated that car, to tell you the truth. Nothing against the Swedes and their sexy blond hair, but we couldn't afford the Saab and it put us under a debt eight ball that never rolled off us.

Or maybe I didn't really hate the car, I hated that Billy bought the damn thing. "Our ship's comin' in, baby," he'd always say, and the crazy part is the guy believed it, no matter how low our tide got or how many storms were in the forecast.

Billy could finance the car because he was working for the power company, reading meters in the Utah sticks, and I was a cashier at the mercantile. It was the closest we ever came to being rich, or at least living like other people. But after a year he got fired for drinking on the job and informing his supervisor that he was an asshole. In case you're wondering, according to Billy the situation was all the boss's fault. Nothing was ever Billy's fault.

Which is why I wonder what he'd say if they'd managed to pull him alive from that one-car wreck outside the Ute reservation. His best friend's wife (you won't hear me say her name) survived in the passenger seat, but unlike Billy she was wearing her belt. Billy always drove like a bat out of hades, but maybe it was an armadillo's fault that he swerved the Saab off the road. Maybe a jackalope jumped onto his windshield or a shiny UFO distracted him.

I know one thing. It definitely would have been my fault if I hadn't kept paying his life insurance premiums.

# Drive Fast, Take Chances

Fitz threw a good party. I only left because I never linger till the downside of anything.

I was nearly to my car when Fitz yelled, "Drive fast, take chances!"

I turned and saw him grinning on the porch, arm around my ex-girlfriend Karen. Despite the potential for awkwardness there was none. We're amicable adults with suitable loose grips on history.

They waved goodbye and I waved back, pondering a response—"Words to live by!"—but decided to swallow it. Karen rested her head on Fitz's shoulder, but not until I drove away. I only saw it in my rearview.

# The Downside of Anything

Fitz throws a good party, and I'm only leaving because it's my policy to never linger till the downside of anything. Since I don't believe in suicide, I realize this resolution might be tested someday.

I'm nearly to my car when Fitz yells behind me, "Drive fast, take chances!"

I turn and see him grinning on his front porch with an arm around the second of my two ex-girlfriends named Karen, both of whom are at the party. Despite the potential for awkwardness there was none; we're all amicable adults with suitable loose grips on history.

They wave goodbye and I wave back, pondering a response—"Words to live by!"—but decide to swallow it. Karen Two rests her head on Fitz's shoulder, but only after I drive away. I see it in my rearview.

Turning the corner, I sort of wish I'd used that "Words to live by!" line. Does *l'esprit de l'escalier* apply when you don't say something you thought of at the time, or only when it comes to you later?

If you're keeping score, which I'm not, I broke up with Karen One, and Karen Two broke up with me, in both cases for all the usual and all the right reasons. No one disputes this; any knots in the stomach or sleepless nights were spawned by vanity, not sense, and the unearned pain was fleeting.

During the drive home I compare the Karens—a dispassionate connoisseur of Karens, sniffing their bouquets, swishing them around in my mouth and spitting them out without drinking them and letting them go to my head. It's not a matter of better or worse, but rather of individual taste, or simply what's on the menu. A lightly chilled Karen One for a twilight stroll on the beach; a well-decanted Karen Two for sharing the Sunday *New York Times*. Neither is a particularly rare vintage, but I'm no snob.

The current trend toward screw tops instead of cork suits me fine.

I'm still mulling over Karens when I reach my condo on Common Place. I know, I know, but it beats a street named for a builder's daughter, like Annie Way where Fitz lives. I step into the living room at a minute past midnight. Even leaving Fitz's before the downside means not getting to bed till the next day. I used to think parties were just revving up as one day slipped into the next, but midnight is starting to matter now that I'm thirty-four.

I strip to my briefs, brush my teeth and curl up in the sheets, but chewed goo from every guacamoled chip I ate at Fitz's feels like it's trapped festering between my teeth, and I have no choice but to get up and floss.

Flicking flecks from between my molars, I notice in the bathroom mirror that my forehead seems bigger. Is it my imagination, or has my hairline begun a slow retreat? I wonder if I'll go bald, and how long it will take. Years, surely, lots of years, if it even happens at all.

Karen Two likes men with shaved heads, thinks it's primal and masculine, but she's from Chicago and has a Michael Jordan complex. I doubt that terrifyingly tattooed skinheads would make her heart flutter, except maybe in fear, but who knows, with women anything's possible.

I toss the limp string in the trash. My great-aunt Eleanor used to rinse floss and use it over and over until it frayed to pieces. Funny, I haven't thought of Auntie Ellie in forever.

I return to bed with a pristine mouth, and lie weirdly and widely awake. Are you serious? Dead beat yet I can't sleep? I spit a curse toward the ceiling and flop on my side. My mother would threaten to wash my mouth out with soap when I swore, but the only time she actually tried to force a cake of Ivory past my lips I bit her finger and tasted sudden blood. That was also the only time she ever hit me, a reaction slap to the head as she yelped in pain. My ear on the pillow remembers the sting.

Suddenly the world seems very big, and life extremely long and unbuttoned. I wonder what's happening at the party, and if either of the Karens will sleep alone tonight. In a way it's a shame to miss out on something, even if it *is* the downside, but what good are principles if you don't stick to them?

# *Gracias* for Bringing It with You

Sighing, Ron Keefe turns away from a stack of *The Scarlet Letter* essays he's been putting off grading. He peers out the window of his dorm parent room, searching in vain for a student's car older than his Mazda.

A scabies epidemic has erupted at Perkins Preparatory Academy. Keefe considers confessing (accidents happen, right?) but how could he maintain classroom authority as Captain Scabies? Not to mention coaching authority, and the parents who'd call for his head impaled on a five-iron.

This is Keefe's second year at Perk Prep. He arrived fresh from college with high hopes and an even higher girlfriend, but Lydia decamped to Taos via Roswell last summer and never returned.

Keefe started wrestling in high school just to do something manly enough to shut up his father, and figured it beat shredding his knees playing football. But he actually enjoyed the sport, and since Perkins needed a wrestling coach, it was a big reason he got this job.

Now it might be why he gets fired. No one has traced the outbreak back to him—yet—but Keefe has little doubt that he donated the scabies mites to some of his wrestlers while demonstrating holds. Which in turn has put the season on hold, because who wants to grapple with a potentially contagious opponent? It's particularly galling since they were on track to be the first Perkins wrestling team with a winning record since Bill Clinton was President.

Keefe ponders his week in Mexico over Christmas break. He had stayed at El Conquistador Luxe Resort, lured by a brochure that turned out to be a shameless welter of equivocal verbiage and Photoshop trickery. In hindsight, the lack of a more recent blurb than one from Sammy Davis, Jr. ("El Conk is a gas, man!") was definitely a red flag.

To add to the fun, his attempt to escape frigid New England

featured temperatures in the fifties the whole week. A rare "north front," Armando the resort manager called it. He flashed a crenellated smile. "*Gracias* for bringing it with you, Señor Keefe."

Keefe attacks his itching crotch like a rat dog digging for a vole. He hopes like hell the tingling in his areolas is psychosomatic. Slipping his hands under his shirt, he cradles his breasts like a pre-pubescent girl checking for growth. His steelworker father's mantra (though of course Big Mike Keefe would never use that pansy word) bounces hard around his brain: "When you get an itch, scratch it." Maybe that explains Big Mike's near-fatal heart attack last July, the day after Lydia left. Well, that and two packs of Camels a day.

Keefe considers a visit to the school nurse. Yeah, right—reveal his humiliating symptoms to Cindy Parker? Drop his Dockers for her to inspect his embarrassment? He'd have zero chance with her after that. Not that he has much chance anyway or would even consider it if Lydia were still here, but Keefe is most definitely not his father, and possesses a mantra of his own: "You never know."

How else to explain the lascivious afternoon he spent in the El Conk honeymoon suite with a voluptuous divorcée from Cleveland? It's a memory to savor, even if Mimi did turn out to be married, and desired Keefe not for his animal charms, but for revenge against her "cheating *pendejo* of a shoe salesman husband."

At least scabies isn't as dire as Keefe's original worry. STD's were a mystery to him, but when ferocious genital itching broke out they certainly seemed like an obvious candidate. He had donned condoms during the frolic in the honeymoon suite's lumpy, heart-shaped bed, but for all he knew Mimi harbored microbes that could burrow through latex. Fortunately, though, even if he had what his father sneeringly called VD, it was his problem alone. Returning to his Perkins celibacy, he hadn't infected anyone else.

Two weeks later he realized he'd been spreading scabies since his return from Mexico.

Keefe drums his fingers on the Hawthorne essays. He slides one off the pile: "*The Scarlet Letter*: An Analization of the Text."

"It's a red-letter day, dude," he whispers, and manages a smile. Fighting not to scratch, he wonders if Lydia will ever come back. He wonders if he even wants her to. He thinks about calling home, about talking to his mother and, inevitably, for a minute or two, his father. It'll probably make him want to scream, but it's not like people are around forever.

# That's Not Funny

# The Hypocritic Oath

My wife is not the sort of person you'd expect to chainsaw the furniture.

She established some ground rules on our first date, nearly five years ago. We were on our second margaritas at Captain Salty's, an oceanfront bar with nets and buoys hanging from the ceiling. A light rain started, just a drizzle, and I suggested a walk on the beach, not because I wanted to, but because I figured she might think it was romantic.

Polly touched my hand, her fingers cool from the glass. "There's something you need to know about me, David. I'm not a hippie. I don't like dancing in the rain."

"So that's a no?"

"A resounding one."

I lifted her hand to my lips, kissed her knuckles. "Staying here sounds like a great idea," I told her. "Let's do it anyway."

One drink later I said, "I can play the guitar, but not the heartstrings. How about you?"

She smiled, sort of. "If we're going to get personal, I need to caution you that I may be habit-forming. And having sex with socks on doesn't bother me at all."

I couldn't resist a glance under the table, though I knew what I'd see. "It's summer. We're wearing sandals."

"What kind of woman do you take me for? Sex with sandals on is out of the question."

"I love a woman who sticks to her principles," I said, looking in her eyes as I licked some salt off the rim of my glass.

So that's how we started. Our relationship was based on weirdness and wordplay, maybe not the ideal foundation, but not the shakiest either. Violence, for instance; violence is worse. And lies. And violent lies.

Come to think of it, suggesting a walk in the rain I didn't want to take can be construed as a lie. Polly's the lawyer; let her debate that. I'm the doctor who took the Hippocratic Oath and pledged that I would "never do harm to anyone." Sleeping with Polly's sister was a bad idea—wrong, if you will—but what was I supposed to do, harm Polly by telling her?

For the record, I'm not the only one who lied. Polly told me, more than once, that she didn't know how to use a chainsaw.

# Religious Holiday

My name is Christian Cohen. My father is a blond Bible Belt Jew, my mother a black Baptist from Brooklyn. I am an atheist. Not a good atheist, not even a practicing one—I make a furtive sign of the cross during airplane turbulence, and pray after routine physicals until the tests come back negative. I skipped work today like I do every Yom Kippur, to breakfast on bacon then spend the day playing, not atoning, though I can't ditch the inkling that there will be hell to pay.

Now it's raining, god damn it. I hate electrical storms, lightning prying like a police searchlight, thunder exploding like the wrath of some vengeful deity primitive people invented. I have no fear, of course—except of losing my ten A.M. tee-time. It's my dog that's whining, cowering under the bed. Not me.

"Be quiet! It's only a little rain, just a little noise."

He must fear the sharpness in my voice, the obvious confidence he wishes he had, because the whimpering increases.

"Shut up!" I yell. "It's not like it lasts forever!"

Before long the last rumble fades. The sun pierces the clouds like those Technicolor rays when Charlton Heston was Moses. My hound emerges hangdog, chastened by his cowardice, ready to fetch a stick, ready for anything. I smile, caution myself about drinking too much coffee. Nerves . . . nerves, that's all.

My feet will get soaked but I will play golf today, the way I was supposed to, the way it was planned. Maybe it was predestined, from the first second of time. Reminding myself to keep my head down, keep my eye on the ball, I curse my fate that I don't believe in predestination.

# Sunflowers of Evil

I was in the Luau Lounge pondering my unpublished destiny when Charles Baudelaire took the stool next to me. "Call me Chuck," he said, grabbing a fistful of *fromage* goldfish crackers in existential resignation.

We talked about romance and poetry, about inspiration and talent and why the Cubs had not won the World Series since 1908.

"Absinthe!" he cried.

"Absinthe makes the heart grow fonder," I said.

The bartender's face needed a nap. "That green swill from Europe? No can do."

"Pernod then, *espèce de con*!"

She emptied Chuck's choked ashtray. "Your lungs must look like fresh asphalt."

Baudelaire gazed at his lap. "My lungs were not the organ that betrayed me."

I steered him away from spirochetes and tincture of mercury. "*The Flowers of Evil*, Chuck. Hell of a book."

The poet tapped his temple. "Forget Valentine's Day just *once*, *mon vieux*, and you'll find out what I meant."

Commotion erupted at the coconut-shell door. The Samoan bouncer held aloft a scowling adolescent in knickers and a beret. Baudelaire guffawed as the kid kicked and squirmed.

"It's that little punk Artie Rimbaud, getting carded!"

"I am the great Rimbaud!"

"If you're Rambo," the Samoan sneered, "I'm Robert Redford."

"I wrote 'The Drunken Boat'!"

"What happens on cruise ships ain't my business. The Luau don't serve minors since the last time they shut us down."

The poet's heaving chest was crisscrossed with bandoliers. "Nobody disses Rimbaud!"

"Yeah, not even the whole Vietnamese army. Now blow."

Rimbaud's eyes lit up, until he realized that meant he was supposed to leave. He flashed a double-barrel bird in our direction.

"You're overrated, Baudelaire! *Reader's Digest* wants your reeking poems!"

Chuck sniffed as if last week's *poisson* had been left under the radiator. "Damn Verlaine for not having better aim when he shot him." Baudelaire oozed negative capability, with a *soupçon* of stoicism for flavor.

The bouncer flung the kid out. Rimbaud's adenoidal whine pierced through a side window.

"Cubs suck, Bawdy Lair! Your poems should be in public toilets, then they'd finally be good for something!"

"He's *vert* with envy because I got another NEA grant," Chuck confided—as if I didn't know already from my umpteenth rejection letter from the same source.

"Yo, Body Hair! I just scored a MacArthur! Sixty grand a year till I'm old enough to vote, and I don't even have to fart for it!"

"*C'est de la politique!*" Chuck spat. "Who does that *petit* worm know on the committee?"

Heated moans blared from the bowels of the Bridges of Madison County pinball game. A figure wearing wooden shoes and earmuffs hunched over the box, masterfully fingering the buttons. Hardly anyone played that machine now, though at one time citizens had inexplicably lined up to feed it vast sums of money, despite the fact that it only gave you two balls. They were enormous balls, though, and constructed of the shiniest brass ever seen.

The pinball warlock furiously racked up points.

"Forty million!" he crowed. "A record! I am an *artiste!*"

Chuck grimaced artistically. "*Mon dieu*, van Gogh, get a grip. It's only a damn game." Then, in a *sotto voce* titter: "Friends, Romans, countrymen, lend me your ear."

Vincent pointed a finger down his throat. "Golly, Evil Flower, that's real original."

"Like painting a vase of sunflowers is *so* cutting edge. Pull your thumb out of the dike and smell the coffee."

"Nice mixed metaphor. You might have a future writing Hallmark cards."

"Yeah, with lame pictures of sunflowers on them. Or skies full of whirlpools like somebody's flushing them down the toilet."

"Spoken like a true bourgeois." Van Gogh gazed starry-eyed at his tally on the machine, the angular four followed by seven plump, insatiable zeroes. "I'm flying to Tokyo tomorrow to do the sets for the new Godzilla film. I have a yen for the serious simoleons those exotic Orientals throw around."

"The lucky *cochon*," Baudelaire whimpered. "Godzilla is almost as brilliant as Jerry Lewis. Is there no end to a poet's pain?"

At least you got the NEA grant, I thought. All I have are enough rejection slips to wallpaper the Moulin Rouge.

Chuck drained his drink. "Man will not merely endure," he said with tears in his eyes, "he will prevail." He stumbled out without looking back.

The bartender slapped the check in front of me.

"What does it matter?" I muttered into my cup. "In a century we'll all be dead, and no one will be reading us anyway."

# Merry Andrew

When Andrew Fenster was fourteen and his mother found him with his tighty whities drooped around his ankles, toying with his boyo while ogling a Victoria's Secret catalogue, Andy figured that at least he'd gotten the most embarrassing experience of his life out of the way.

That theory has been frequently tested over the next seven years, most recently last Saturday night.

Like the time his mother gaped aghast at his zestful self-abuse, this incident started out pleasantly enough. Carli Ruggiero had enthusiastically accepted his offer to dine chez Taco Bell before a concert by Sedated, a Ramones tribute band. "I adaw Spanish food!" she gushed in a Brooklyn accent so extreme it seemed the product of a community theater ham from Omaha.

"Cool," Andy said, and it was, especially when Carli hardly needed a prod to accompany him to his dorm room after the ear-bleeding show.

Andy locked the door, feeling the power of his "I Wanna Get Laid Shirt," a gaudy Hawaiian number he figured oozed equal measures of insouciance and savoir-faire—not that his vocabulary included either term.

"Beer, Carli?"

"Does a beah shit in the woods?"

The mini-fridge was emptier than his roommate's soul.

"Goddamn Fugelsang stole my PBR!"

"I'll castrate the bastahd," Carli promised.

He sat next to her, thighs touching. Soon she was unbuttoning the IWGL Shirt, he was unzipping her jeans, and they were easing into his bed.

"What the—?" Carli threw back the sheet. "Ahhh, you scummah! A used rubbah!"

She plucked the wrinkled condom from her leg and flung it in Fenster's face before fleeing.

"I had no choice, dude," Fugelsang explained after stumbling in at two. "Cindy bled on my sheets last week and I didn't want to scare Kathy off. I'll replace the beer."

Fenster fantasized garroting Fugelsang's pimply throat. "You left a scumbag in my bed!"

"My bad. But I doubt it leaked. I didn't turn it inside out or anything. If it makes you feel any better, Kathy was an absolute animal in the rack."

Smiling anemically, Fenster pondered his single, meager consolation: Fugelsang's funky surprise when he turned over his pillow.

# Tongue Lashing

How was I to know *Tongue Lashing* was a porn flick? I played it thinking it might help me apologize for what I said. To my surprise she was curious, not contemptuous; soon we weren't watching anymore, though the soundtrack played sexy soul for us.

I guess we're good again.

# Kentucky Jelly

"Kentucky Jelly? What's that?"

I grin at Lucy's cleverness, but it flattens out when I see her frowning at the K-Y Jelly on the Walgreens shelf. Good God, is she serious?

I glance around. We're alone in our aisle. "It's like Tennessee Jam, only slipperier."

"Which one tastes better? In your opinion."

"Depends what you put it on, I guess."

Lucy smiles like autumn sunshine. "What do *you* like it on?"

"To be honest, I prefer not using a condiment. I like things unadulterated."

"Good," she says, reaching for a big tube. "I wouldn't think of breaking the sixth commandment."

# The End of the After

As Claire unscrews the wine cap, Rick peers at her bookshelf. "*The End of the After*. Clever title."

It's *Affair*, you nitwit, not *After*. But he paid for dinner and has a nice smile, and at least he noticed the books.

"It's my favorite," she says, pouring their glasses full.

# K Pasa

My blind date wants to meet at K Pasa, a dorky name for a restaurant if I've ever heard one, especially since the food there isn't even Mexican. I'm not sure what it is, Polish maybe, or Jamaican. Something un-American.

She probably plans on breaking up with me. Ignorant people claim that can't happen on a first date, but I know better because it has happened to me, and more than once—twice, to be exact, which I pride myself on being. Precision counts in this world. Otherwise, we might as well live in a zoo. I know what you're thinking—ha, ha, this world *is* a zoo—and all I can say is ha, ha, you might be right, but I don't live my life that way.

One good thing about K Pasa, at least I can walk to it and not waste money on an Uber. It's only a mile and there's sidewalk half the way. I'll get there early and if my shirt is sticking to my back, I'll duck into Pinky's Liquors across the parking lot and dry off in his arctic AC. I'll peruse the champagne section and watch the window. With any luck I'll see her drive in. Odds are she has some terminally cute car like a yellow VW bug. She'll check her makeup in the rearview, because they always do, right? Then I'll know she's meeting someone, and odds are it's me. When she walks in alone—smoothing the skirt on her flanks? tossing back her casually perfect hair?—I'll leave Pinky's empty-handed, with a casual mention that they don't carry the vintage I'd sought.

Should I shave? The Internet says a two-day beard makes women's hormones kick in, they can't help it, but mine is three days going on four so there might be diminishing returns. Love is a complex thing to navigate, and I don't care what the chat room experts say, most of the voyage is in uncharted waters. I break out the Barbasol.

OK, smooth as a baby's butt for Sugar Lips. If I have a beer now that will be one less I'll be tempted to purchase at K Pasa's undoubtedly inflated prices. I wonder if she's the type to order the most expensive thing on the menu, insist on going Dutch, or somewhere in-between. There's $96.47 in my debit account, so I'm good unless she spends like a Kardashian. If that happens, the least she can do is chip in.

Why did she pick K Pasa? She mentioned something about reading a review, but you know how women ramble on, if you paid attention to everything they say you'd be as crazy as they are. Maybe her uncle or somebody owns the place and she's trying to keep the sinking ship in business, though in that case we might at least get a free dessert or appetizer.

I'll take this can of PBR for the walk. I'd hate to lose the deposit, but maybe I'll find a bush to stash it behind and pick it up on my way back. That is, if she doesn't hand me the keys to her car to drive us to her place for unbridled carnality till dawn.

Hey, it could happen. From a law-of-averages perspective, the universe might decide that I'm due for such an eventuality.

Put the Binaca bottle in your pants pocket, even if it does make a suggestive bulge. Masking beer breath is worth the awkwardness. If she says, "Is that a Binaca bottle in your pocket or are you just happy to see me?" you'll probably need both of the prophylactics in your wallet tonight. Think of a witty comeback to that line during the walk to K Pasa.

Well, that beer disappeared in a hurry. This one for the road tastes even better. Damn, barely to the sidewalk and I need to go back and pee again. Is it going to be one of those nights? Trip after embarrassing trip to the K Pasa pissoir? She'll probably smile and make some snide remark about Flomax.

To hell with that garbage. I've got three more PBR's, a pack of hotdogs and my favorite self for company. I exit the bathroom and turn on the tube. Say what you like about me, but I'm no fool.

The bitch was probably going to break up with me anyway.

# Second Acts

# People Are Idiot's

Morgan stares at the Facebook page, fingers drumming on his thigh. Doing nothing is one option, and possibly the best one. Anyone can make an inadvertent error. But this doesn't feel inadvertent. This feels smug and stupid, and if it doesn't exactly break Morgan's heart, it does trample hopes he has dared to let build for the last twenty-six days.

If a relationship can't survive a couple being Facebook friends, then it's hopeless, right? Face facts and move on. But Morgan likes Vanessa, a lot, as in he might actually love her, and for reasons far beyond physical attraction—though the sex is the best he's ever known, hands down and everywhere else hands can end up.

But "People are idiot's"? The screwed-up plural is one thing; chances are he has done worse, without noticing (because if he'd noticed he would have fixed it). It's the comment itself that troubles him, a response to a post supporting universal background checks for gun buyers. Morgan searches for ambiguity, but it's hard to conclude otherwise than that Vanessa's "idiot's" are people like him, the over 90% (he googled it) of Americans who want universal background checks.

Who could be against keeping potentially dangerous people from getting firearms? Supposedly, even most NRA members support background checks. How are they possibly an idiotic idea? Morgan considers adding a comment to the thread, but words fail him, and so does courage. Besides, he knows it's an exercise in futility. Most people's minds are made up.

His isn't.

He closes his eyes as a memory ten years old pops into view: day one of his freshman comp class at a huge state university, taught by a surprisingly hot graduate student. Morgan congratulated himself on his luck as she went over the syllabus. Then, on the middle of page two, she reached her "Plajerism" policy.

He figured she'd blush at her mistake and make some witty

remark that would cement his crush on her. But she just read the section and moved on to her attendance policy.

There was no way he'd say anything in class, but Morgan debated going up to her afterward. He even took a few steps toward the lectern where she stood, but half a dozen students already hovered around her. He wondered if one of them would mention the error. He wondered if anyone else in the class even *knew* it was an error.

Morgan left without a word. He never did tell her. In the end he had to admit she made him a better writer--though it rankled when he got a B from someone who couldn't spell "plagiarism." For the record, she also said "like" too often.

Nearly a month since their first date, and until three minutes ago Morgan had marveled at how he and Vanessa liked the same things. *Citizen Kane* and *Plan 9 from Outer Space*. *The Great Gatsby* and gin gimlets. Tofu burritos and veggie burgers perversely topped with bacon. Staying in bed till noon on Sundays, but hardly sleeping after waking at nine.

Politics? He can't remember if they've discussed politics, which seems semi-impossible now that he thinks about it. That stuff always comes up, right? Unless it doesn't. Unless there are so many better things to talk about.

One topic that had come up (On their first date? No, the second.) was *30 Rock*. They both loved the show. Morgan takes heart. If Vanessa were channeling Ann Coulter she couldn't stand Alec Baldwin, right? She had especially liked the "Dealbreakers" episode, to the point of quoting some of Tina Fey's lines, and Morgan had cracked up.

Now he's starting to feel the other meaning of "crack up." Morgan knows that's melodramatic; he's not losing his mind, just the sense of rightness with the world he has felt since his first five minutes with Vanessa. He has never clicked so completely with a woman before. His four years with Ginny after college never felt like more than good fun, and when the fun faded it was a fairly easy kiss goodbye for both of them. So much more is at stake now, despite their short time together.

Gnawing his lip, more nervous than before their first date, he types, "Idiots are people too." He stares at the words for nearly a minute before deleting them. He substitutes, "Some of my best friends are idiots," and adds a smiley-face emoji.

Feeling like a moron, and like he has no choice, Morgan hits the return key.

# Visible Human

Two things happened to me the day I learned about the Visible Human Project, which cut an executed murderer's body into 1,871 slices. Not slices like a deli salami; they'd grind away a millimeter, take photos then grind off another millimeter, leaving only a holy mess and the photographic evidence. I'm not sure which end they started on, but somehow I hope it was the feet.

So, the two things. I used the last address label with both Becky's and my name on it, and a shithead with a wonderful wife and boozy breath told me, "I envy your freedom."

# Memorial

I went to plenty of anti-Vietnam War rallies at Berkeley. I believed in the cause and would have gone even if I hadn't, because that's where the action was. Most of my friends were there, and a fair crowd of faculty. Once my history professor even passed me a fat joint that was making the rounds, his touch on my shoulder and smoke-filled-lungs croak of "Here, man" warming my insides for the way it showed he was treating me like an equal. If I tried that with one of my students now, I'd probably get my pink slip in a jail cell.

I was thinking about those rallies when I went to the Vietnam Memorial in 1977, on a hot, sticky midsummer night. It was only right, Janie said, that our first meeting with the monument be in the dark. My hand found hers as we stepped slowly down the flagstones, numbed, overwhelmed by name after dead name carved in stark black rock, row after row forever like headstones in Arlington Cemetery. To my surprise dozens of other people were there, of all ages, as silent as mourners at a wake pausing before the casket, then moving on.

"You were right," I said in a near-whisper as we walked toward the Lincoln Memorial. "Night was better."

"What an awful time, Ricky. What an awful time it was."

"Yeah." I thought of my brother, recently returned from years in Canada after President Carter pardoned draft evaders. I thought of my father's blind belief in his country, and of a girl who got me involved with "the movement" at Berkeley and was now my wife, leaning lightly against my side. Our divorce was nearly a decade away.

"But there were great times, too." I pulled her closer. Even at ten P.M. two tour buses were at the Lincoln Memorial, with their engines running.

"Of course," she said. "I met you." Her voice sounded strange. When I looked at her, she was crying, just a little.

I kept my tears in. "And there weren't any discos, babe. That's enough right there if you ask me."

She smiled, just a little, and that was enough right then. We climbed the stairs to read the Gettysburg Address carved in white marble, with no pigeon on Lincoln's head at this hour of the night.

# Mixture

"Sex and violence don't mix. Why waste good violence on sex?" I look for a smile; I feel it in his words. But Roger—my best friend as a kid, best man at my wedding six years ago—is concentrating too hard to smile. He's staring down the barrel of his 30.06, waiting for that snapping turtle to stick his head above water again. He doesn't want it eating the game fish in his pond. I've seen him shoot half a dozen since junior high.

"I never hit her," he says evenly. "I never hit her even once."

"Of course you didn't."

"I don't know what makes her say that, Donny."

Roger never uses Carla's name since she left. But she's not a "cheating bitch" or "worthless whore" either, like some other friends' ex-wives—or my own, once or twice, when pain won out over pride.

"Come on, don't worry about it. Nobody believes her." The lie feels like dirt on my tongue.

I like Carla. She's smart, and secure enough about it that even in high school she didn't play dumb. One time she told me of a nightmare Roger had, years after he got back from Vietnam. He was writhing on his stomach, she said, whimpering over and over *Burning people smell so bad* without waking up.

"I didn't dare touch him," she said. She put her hand on my arm. "You're the only one I've told this to. Not even him." Carla stared off at nothing, nodding slowly. She shrugged. "Especially not him."

Roger's finger is tight on the trigger. Suddenly he looks away from his target, straight at me.

"Remember when we were kids, and found that dead bullfrog on the other side of the pond? Nailed down on a stump?"

I nod. I can still see that spread-eagle frog, belly-up and leathery black from the sun, its gut a squirming ball of maggots. It gave me nightmares for a week.

Roger takes aim again, out across the water.

"I didn't do that," he says.

# Animal Cruelty

On their second date Yantz goes to Sandy's house for dinner, which he doesn't necessarily consider the best of all possible options. The first date was certainly fun, a spirited segue from overpriced caffeine at Starbucks to chilled chardonnay and two hours of nakedness at his apartment. Dinner isn't the problem; Sandy probably cooks like nobody's business, and Yantz loves salmon. He brought the chardonnay, same brand she liked so much last weekend.

But isn't it a bit soon to meet her kid?

Sandy thinks ten-year-old Natalie is adorable, and said as much several times during the public portion of date number one, though the child was never mentioned again once their clothes hit the floor.

The girl seems to share her mother's opinion about her adorableness. Natalie looks like a clone of Shirley Temple—Shirley Temple with braces and a pink iPhone, that is. Yantz half-expects to be subjected to "The Good Ship Lollipop," though maybe in an ear-assaulting version inspired by Nicki Minaj.

"What grade are you in?" Yantz asks, figuring he's obligated to pretend to care.

"Fifth," she announces, blonde curls bouncing as she starts hopping up and down for no apparent reason.

"Oh really?" Yantz could gag at how phony he sounds, but Sandy is beaming at him.

"Yes. I love school. For Miss Martin's class I'm doing a report on animal cruelty."

Yantz can't help himself. "For or against?"

The hopping stops. Natalie's jaw drops and sort of palpitates, like a fish with no flop left in it quivering on the floor of a boat. Though his chances of ever kissing that birthmark on Sandy's thigh again have probably plummeted to zero, Yantz only semi-regrets the remark.

To his amazement, Sandy starts to laugh. She laughs so hard it's almost unnerving. "That's hil*ar*ious! I didn't know you were so funny!"

Yantz didn't know it either. His sense of humor, when acknowledged at all, is generally described as dry to the point of aridity. "Saharan," the previous woman he had been dating described it, the same night she said she thought they should start seeing other people.

"Isn't Kenny funny, Nat?"

Kenny? He's been Ken to her up till now. Yantz is no grammar expert, but in his experience when women call you by a diminutive, for them it's a form of the possessive. The weird thing is that he doesn't resent it. It feels borderline wonderful to be wanted by a woman who thinks he's funny, who uses a diminutive for her daughter in the same sentence she uses one for him.

Natalie's smile is tentative but still pure Shirley Temple, right down to the dimples that are, well, if not adorable, certainly cute.

Sandy is cutting the foil off the wine bottle.

"So, Natalie," Yantz says, "your report sounds pretty interesting."

Her smile grows and glows. Yantz imagines reading the report, nodding thoughtfully, maybe even helping her. He imagines reading stories to a kid on the couch with her weary head on his shoulder.

Where the hell did that come from? Can life actually work this way?

Sandy hands him a glass. "Cheers," she says, their eyes meeting for a long time, but nowhere near as long as Yantz suddenly wants to be familiar with her hidden birthmark and other secrets.

Natalie eyes them both, caught somewhere between wisdom and wonder. "My report's mostly about cruelty to chickens."

Sandy's hand gently squeezes his shoulder. For half a moment Yantz closes his eyes.

"That's terrible, Nat," he says. "Tell me more."

# Ghost Broccoli

I wasn't a picky eater as a child, so I'm not thrilled when Charlie comes over every other weekend and refuses to eat things I wish he would, like the eggplant parmesan I cooked tonight. It's practically lasagna, right? He loves lasagna.

"I'll fry you some turkey dogs if you at least try the cauliflower."

His face twists in melodramatic horror. The kid could have acted for D.W. Griffith.

"Ghost broccoli? Gross!"

Kara finishes tossing the salad. We've only been seeing each other for six weeks, and this is her first time with my nine-year-old son. Kara's wonderful, and I want her to feel the same about me. Parenting like a stand-up comic dealing with a heckler isn't my best strategy.

She sets the tongs in the bowl and picks up her wine glass by the stem. I always notice how a person holds a wine glass. I don't judge; I notice.

"Ghost broccoli," she says. "That's pretty clever, Charlie. Did you make it up or did you hear it somewhere?"

He shrugs, trying to hide that he's pleased, but a little smile happens.

"I don't know. Made it up, I guess."

My son's not usually a wordplay kind of kid, so I have my doubts about his claim. But I've never heard "ghost broccoli" before, so who knows? I make a mental note to google it later, though as usual I'll probably forget.

"You know how cauliflower's really good?" Kara says. "Put some soy sauce and parmesan cheese on it. Want to try that with me?"

Charlie's not stupid; he knows he's getting played. But he's also getting attention.

Looking at the floor he says, "I guess."

His second "I guess" in thirty seconds. I almost mention it, but not wanting to second guess yet again my actions as a parent, I keep quiet—though I smile at my unintentional pun. Second guess…très witty, bucko.

"What's so funny, dad?"

Kara's waiting for my answer too, with a soft smile of her own. Somehow, I get the feeling she knows exactly why I'm smiling. That's impossible, obviously, but I like it.

I pick up my wine glass, by the stem. "Just playing a little guessing game with myself."

Charlie squints at me. "That's weird."

"What's wrong with weird?" I tell him. "Normal's boring."

Of course, like most kids—hell, like most everybody—Charlie wants to fit in. Normal is safe. Don't I want him to be safe? I think of the "Keep Austin Weird" tee shirt Charlie's mother bought me during a business trip to Texas the year before he was born. I wonder where it is, if I even still have it. I wonder if it still fits.

Kara asks, "Have you heard of the golden mean, Charlie?"

"My mom says don't be mean." He glances my way. "Dad too."

I wonder how tough our divorce is on him, this shuttling between parents. I have nothing to go on. My parents' fortieth anniversary is next month, and I've hardly ever even seen them argue. Charlie didn't sign up for any of this. Then again, none of us signed up to be on this planet in the first place.

"The golden mean is different," Kara says. "It's when you find the perfect balance between things."

"That doesn't sound mean," Charlie says, but I rejoice in his tone: he sounds like he trusts her.

I do, too. Not even two months together, and I'm pretty sure Kara is The One. But I thought that about Charlie's mother.

For Christ's sake, will you stop acting like a seventh grader and just use Jenna's name?

"So, you're having some cauliflower." I try to make it a statement, not a question.

"It's good to try new things," Kara says, eyes smiling at me over her wine glass. Given her bedroom inventiveness to this point, speculation about what new things she has in mind makes me glad Charlie sleeps like an anvil. Kara's not staying here tonight—it's way too soon for Charlie to experience that—but he'll be in bed at 8:30.

"You're not my mother," he says.

My heart plummets. "What did you tell us about being mean?"

"That's not mean, it's just real."

"Yes, but—"

"Of *course* it's real," Kara says, gripping her glass in both hands.

Yes, it *is* real, as real the trembling edge to my lover's voice and the sudden, shameful possibility that her happiness means more to me than my son's.

# Just One Rule

Heffernan wasn't my friend, just a guy I used to work with, and I hadn't seen him in three years when he emailed to ask if I'd be his best man. Really, dude? Email? Like a sap I said OK.

He started bugging me about a bachelor party, which I hadn't bargained on. I found a hall where a woman told me, "There's just one rule—no dope smoking outside. I don't want any cops in here."

Heffernan was pissed that I didn't hire a stripper. He was distant at the wedding, and his much younger wife smiled too hard.

# A Single Thing

I don't remember what the Japanese exchange student did, just what she said about it when my girlfriend told her how brave she was: "Not brave, just reckless." Midori's English was basic and her accent thick, but I never forgot those words and her sunny smile when she spoke them.

It's been twenty years since I last visited that girlfriend, both of us relieved when I boarded the train west. I waved from the window and never saw her again.

So why does it hurt tonight that I can't recall a single thing she ever said to me with a smile?

# Dry Dream

I've been thinking about Ann today. I suppose it's not that weird to have an old lover pop into your mind, though she's been out of my life for what, eight years? Nine? And it didn't end well. Maybe the best that can be said for our split was that each of us wanted it as bad as the other.

It wasn't nostalgia that brought Ann back. Sure, we had lots of good times before things fell apart, but pining for those days is not part of the equation. Life is far better now. I love Rebecca, she loves me, and I want to keep it that way.

No, what brought Ann back was not nostalgia, but two words: dry dream. Why those words knocked on memory's door is a mystery; I only know that they did, yesterday while Rebecca and I were making love. If it had been during any other time, I doubt they would have stuck. But during sex with your wife on a Sunday afternoon? Of course I remembered. And of course I said nothing to Becca.

Ann came up with "dry dream." She was always inventing clever stuff like that, puns and such. I don't recall the context or when she first said it, but it soon became her catchphrase for anything that seemed promising but would likely go wrong. It was equally useful to describe something that had already failed.

I used "dry dream" too, on occasion, and eventually so did most of our friends. Somehow, though, it always felt like stealing. For better or worse, the phrase belonged to Ann.

It came back to me this morning on my drive to work, "dry dream" a mental retort to some politician prevaricating on NPR. I might have even said it out loud, at least in a whisper. Then at the office I did something unusual for me: I checked for Ann on Facebook, feeling not sleazy exactly, because it wasn't, but maybe a bit like I was reading someone's diary without asking. I sipped my cooling coffee and told myself it was Facebook, for crying out loud; if I'm reading her diary, it's because she left it open on the kitchen counter.

She wasn't on Facebook, at least under the name that I knew. There were a dozen or more with her name, but they were definitely not my Ann. "My"? I took that as a sign and didn't google her name—until lunch. It was a waste of time. It's weird how a particularly unique, interesting person can get lost in a herd sharing a common name. I'm nowhere near as interesting, but my unusual name pops right up in an Internet search. There aren't that many of us around.

I wonder if Ann has ever googled me. If so, she obviously decided to stay disconnected. That's probably for the best. Let napping canines repose. Lame, right? Not clever like something Ann would come up with.

Rebecca usually groans when I make puns, and I don't blame her. I'm no wordsmith like Ann, and my feeble attempts often embarrass me before they're halfway out of my mouth. Not that Becca's any great shakes in the inventiveness department, which is fine. I didn't marry her to entertain me, I married her because I love her.

I never wanted to marry Ann.

Of course, I was younger then; I didn't want to marry anyone. I did want to have sex a lot, though, and Ann was a kindred spirit in that regard, so we got along great until our expectations of each other extended beyond getting naked as often as possible. To be honest, it was mostly Ann's expectations that grew; getting naked as often as possible was still enough for me. But I was with the person who invented "dry dream." She was just with me.

Rebecca knows about Ann, a few facts like I know about Jeremy, Bruce, Peter, Dave #1 and Dave #2. Not that it matters, but for the record my law practice is going gangbusters and I make more than any of them except possibly Dave #1, who inherited Daddy's company. That's not why Becca loves me, but let's face it, it can't hurt.

The next chance I get, I'm going to say "dry dream" to her. Probably she'll roll her eyes: "Seriously, Michael? What does that even *mean*?" Maybe, though, just maybe, my wife will love her plagiarist husband a little more than before, even a little more than she thought possible.

# Pretty Good Americans

# Vaporware

So I sell vaporware for a living—what's that prove? The money's decent, and maybe the stuff will work the way the company hopes, the way I guarantee my customers. You can't hang me for giving it a shot. This is America, last I heard.

A woman leaves me messages, text and voice. She insists she still loves me, uses words like "anodyne" and "inevitable"—but then why'd she move 751 miles away with my brother? I answer the messages. I wrote a postcard saying this is ridiculous. On the other side were "Greetings from Colorado" and a Jackalope the size of a bull. She gave it to me years ago, during a "cute" period. Cute was *her* word. I trust "cute" about as far as I can spit an eight ball.

So here I sit, naked, taking a day off from peddling vaporware. I drank coffee till noon, beer after that, watched two Steve Martin movies and read half an inch of *The Executioner's Song*. I'd bet the farm that postcard arrived today; she'll plan to give herself time to think it over but won't make it past sundown. I debate whether to put in *The Jerk*. My phone starts playing "Sergeant Pepper's Lonely Hearts Club Band." Our song. It stops. I wait, fingers drumming to the silent Beatles beat, then check my voicemail.

"You return my present to tell me I'm not worth a few roaming charges? I'm not that easy to erase. I love you and don't you forget it. This is the twenty-first century, lover. This is America, last I heard."

# Collecting Trollopes

English department nerds inhabit the same campus but a different planet than science nerds. At a faculty event this afternoon involving wine paid for by the taxpayers, I wittily remarked that, "I collect Trollopes." Several pairs of scientific eyebrows rose. Silent sanctimony filled the air. After a pause—awkward on their part, pregnant on mine—I added, "First editions!" (For the record, I do have a *The Way We Live Now* first edition in halfway respectable condition.)

One would expect mirth to have ensued. One would be mistaken. Violet Merkin, astrophysicist and marathon runner, nearly choked on her carrot stick.

"Considering what happened with that adjunct piano teacher last semester, Jeffrey, I find that rather tasteless."

Violet likely has never heard of the Victorian novelist Anthony Trollope, despite her Victorian sensibility. I suppose I should be grateful she at least knows what a trollop is. As for my other interlocutors, Ed Hayes from chemistry and Marcie somebody, a new hire in physics who looked as young as our students, I had my doubts. Their disapproval might just have been an academic version of Stockholm Syndrome.

Talking to Violet always makes me think of those "My Kid Beat Up Your Honor Student" bumper stickers. "Just some English department humor," I said, edging away toward the bar. "What we might call a dollop of Trollope."

The piano teacher (to my dismay, I never met the woman) had been canned for canoodling with a student, about which I feel profoundly ambivalent. Faculty-student "dating" or "relationships" (insert preferred euphemism here) are verboten these days, because of the inherent power difference (not, God forbid, "differential") between the participants. Makes sense. But I have a student who's a good friend of the "victim" (as the newspapers called him), and he says the only trauma the kid felt was from losing the most entertaining piano lessons of his life. Colleges used to have plenty of professors married to their ex-students, and some of those marriages lasted. Now they can't happen, which amounts to one less possibility in your life.

As I handed my plastic cup to the bartender for another infusion of Merlot, Megan O'Connor crept into my mind. Why at that moment? Aren't memories supposedly triggered by something? I hadn't thought of Megan for a month or seen her for twelve years, since that Friday night we drank a pint of vodka at her studio apartment and I turned down her offer to stay over, wanting our first sex to be special, not drunken fumbling we'd forever associate with vicious hangovers. Instead, I tried to drive home, an action that encompassed the two worst decisions of my life: I was arrested for DUI, and when I called her on Sunday Megan said her boyfriend from home had proposed, and she was getting married.

This happened at a large state university, where I was a grad student teaching a section of creative writing and Megan was a senior biology major taking the class "for fun." She was by far the best writer in the group, and a serious student as well, which led to increasingly frequent visits to my office, which led to...well, in the end to nothing but regrets for the road not taken (not to mention the road taken, considering that damn DUI).

A graduate student lives in the grayest of areas when it comes to relationships with students. You *are* a student, after all, except for one class a term the school gives you to teach, saving money by paying you a small fraction of what a professor earns. But in that class you *are* the professor, with a professor's power and responsibilities over students often hardly younger, and sometimes older, than you are. I waited till the semester ended; the day after I gave Megan an A I gave her a call. We met for coffee and I never smiled so much in my life. Two weeks later came the drunken night that changed everything—and absolutely nothing.

Maybe Megan is a college professor now. That was her plan, after all. Maybe she sips wine at university functions, a science nerd communing with nerds from math, history, philosophy—and

English. Maybe, every once in a long while, she remembers the English nerd who rejoiced to see half a dozen Trollope paperbacks on her bookshelves, who will never forget the worry on her face as he bumped the car behind him before pulling out into the damp, empty street.

# Dive

I'm back by the pool table in Shank's, a dive on the wrong side of downtown, trying not to yawn or stare at the chest of a girl in a tight T-shirt babbling about her ex-boyfriend. Suddenly glass shatters, louder than "Freebird" wailing on the jukebox.

I turn and see a hulking lug with a blond mullet brandishing a broken beer bottle like some perverse microphone. It happens so fast you might think I don't have time to be scared, but you'd be wrong. Fistfights are one thing, a goon waving jagged glass quite another. Entertainment value is compromised when you're worried your own blood might join the stains on the floor, and a sneering Neanderthal in a #69 football jersey is slashing the air with a lethal weapon ten feet away. A stringy gnome in a tank top faces him, pool cue on his shoulder like a Little Leaguer hoping he'll draw a walk and not have to swing the bat.

The girl clutches my arm, acquainting me with the copious contents of her shirt. I'm fine with that development as long as it doesn't imply responsibility on my part.

"Hey!" the bartender yells. "There's people barefoot in here!"

The genius with the bottle looks down and realizes he's one of those people. "Fuck me," he philosophizes, gingerly adjusting his stance. I can read the name on his jersey, only partially obscured by his greasy mullet: D. GENERATE.

"Lonnie, we cool?" inquires Mr. Generate.

Relief shines in the scraggly dude's face like he's just been thrown ball four. He nods and relaxes his grip on the stick.

"We cool, Darryl. I don't know why you was so pissed off anyway."

"I *wasn't* pissed off, you fuckhead. It pisses me off when you say stupid shit like that."

"He kind of reminds me of my ex-boyfriend," the girl says. To my surprise she's still holding my arm.

"Who would come in this establishment barefoot?" I ask.

"Why are we here at all?"

I pause to reflect whether she means Shank's, or the universe: location versus ontology. The smart money's on Shank's.

"Damn good question," I say.

"You're funny. You remind me of my ex-boyfriend."

Do I know her name? Not that I care, unless of course she's told it to me, which could prove awkward later on. If she enjoys slumming at Shank's, maybe she'll consider continuing the low-life experience at my hovel (christened The Swamp, its name earned fair and square). This afternoon I changed my sheets and scrubbed the toilet for just such an eventuality. I even considered vacuuming, but there are limits to my hospitality. I compromised and vacuumed my room, though the archipelago of orange candle wax on the carpet is permanent.

I ponder what it would be like to have someone like D. Generate come to the door to pick up your daughter. Would he call you "sir"? Would she beam and say, "Daddy, this is D. He has a Camaro and can bench-press 300 pounds. Isn't he dreamy?"

I decide to take the plunge. "Do you want to maybe get out of here? I have a bottle of Mateus in the fridge." Actually, it's my roommate's, but close enough.

"Unopened?" she asks.

I have no idea if it's open or not. "Of course. What do you take me for?"

Since she's still latched onto my arm, I figure odds are decent she'll stay that way if I start walking. I wonder how old she is, whether she got in with a fake I.D. Not that Shank's is famous for checking. I wonder what my mother would think if she saw me right now, three weeks shy of my thirtieth birthday.

A waitress is approaching with a dustpan and broom, but we're already heading for the exit. Glass crunches under my feet. I don't look down.

# Digestion

I was strolling the fairgrounds, two bites into a deep-fried Twinkie, when I saw a cow with a hole in her side. I'm not sure which of her four stomachs was exposed for our edification, but it was gruesomely educational. A grinning boy turned away from the churning silage and eyed my Twinkie.

# Pedalphiles

Our cycling club's name was definitely not my idea. It's amazingly tone-deaf, actually. But Pedalphiles has some of the best riders in the state, and even more important, it has Jenny Miller, so when they invited me to join I didn't think twice.

OK, that's a total lie. I've lost count of the number of times I've thought about it.

This isn't political correctness from some tiny-testicled liberal. I'm a registered Republican, and no one means any harm by the name Pedalphiles. When the club was founded during Eisenhower's presidency, a word meaning "lovers of pedaling" was clever, not controversial. After all, it was an era with a kid called Beaver on prime time TV.

The issue isn't political correctness—it's that I was molested for two years as an altar boy. I'm one of the damaged kids finally paid off by the Church (somehow, I still have to use that capital "C") after years of stonewalling and fighting in courts. I once heard a guy joke, "For that kind of dough I'd do whatever padre pervert wanted," but no amount of money could erase the taste of that man of God from my life.

I've broken the ice with Jenny, though it's not melting as quickly as I'd like. Being on the same team is a start, not a solution. After all, out of a dozen altar boys at Saint Succotash's (I can't say the real name—part of the court settlement), Father Creepysmile only targeted me. I'll never know how I lost that lottery. Creepysmile said it was because I was special, and through him Jesus loved me even more than my parents did. Since my parents didn't even love each other by then, that sort of made sense, no weirder than some of the gospel stories Creepysmile read to the congregation during Mass. Not to mention the cannibalism of Communion, when he would transform wafers and wine into our Savior's flesh and blood for us to consume like the Lord's own Donner Party.

Creepysmile always closed his eyes as he raised the Host up

toward heaven. Ringing the altar bell after the words "This is my body, which will be given up for you," I'd think of other times he'd close his eyes, gently humming at first, then panting and groaning until he croaked a choking sound like he was being strangled. Often he'd give me a few dollar bills afterward, which I suspect came from the collection basket. He said not to spend more than one or two at a time, so nobody would ask where I got the money. (I was pretty sure "nobody" meant my parents, but I doubt they were paying attention anyway.) He'd ruffle my hair and remind me how much Jesus loved me, and that I shouldn't share our special secret with anyone but God, which I never did because of course God already knew.

I debate about telling my secret to Jenny. Could I share my life with a woman who doesn't know? Crazy question, maybe, considering I've shared nothing with Jenny so far except teammate-style pleasantries, and smiles and high-fives after races. Yesterday's high-five, though...I swear she maintained skin contact longer than usual, longer than for anyone else on the team. Or was that just me holding on to something that wasn't there, holding on to nothing?

It's not small talk material, that's certain. Starbucks (which I'll suggest for our first date, once I raise the courage) likely isn't the place for that sort of revelation. Looking at it objectively I should probably wait until after we've had sex, until we've made that commitment to each other. I've heard the third date is when that usually happens, but I'll be careful not to rush things. I just want to be with Jenny. If it takes till the fourth or even fifth date, that's fine with me.

I wonder if she's had many partners. "Partners" makes it sound like a business transaction but saying "lovers" makes my heart hurt. Besides, after Creepysmile I'm not sure I can trust the word "love" ever again.

I do love to pedal, though, joyfully pumping with Jenny as we climb together, breathing hard, feeling the whole bad world fade as her face, contorted with lovely effort, smiles for me as we hit the finish line. I've never felt so close to anyone, and I'd pray, if only I still could, that words will be my savior and someday come to rescue us.

# Red, Red, Red

We cheerleaders chanted to the helmeted heroes, "Kick 'em in the stomach, kick 'em in the head! We want blood, red, red, red!" A year later my quarterback got shot through the helmet in Vietnam and I was chanting to LBJ, asking how many kids he had killed that day.

# Field Trip

The woman holding court at the Tiki Lounge wore a shocking pink T-shirt, the word MANIAC stretched tight across her chest in black block letters with silver sequins. I was impressed. I was young.

"People take themselves too seriously," she said, tendrils of smoke snaking from her nostrils. "Especially comedians."

People laughed—seriously, they did. They raised cool glasses to their lips, dragged deep on cigarettes, carefully choreographed chance body contact that was anything but. I would have too, but I didn't want to show that I was eavesdropping. I was too cool for that. It was summer and I had just graduated from high school. The names meant nothing to me then, but Woodstock was two months away, Altamont six, the invasion of Cambodia almost a year. As it turned out, I would miss the first two.

The woman squeezed a pale, chubby guy's fleshy chin as if it belonged to an irresistible infant. Crow's feet of pleasure furrowed around his eyes. She leaned so close she could have kissed him.

"I'd be good," she said, "if I wasn't so bad at it."

Everyone shrieked with delight. I was mute. The guy must have smelled her breath, but the crow's feet did not fly away. They acted like they belonged there. The way I belonged there. I'd turned eighteen in April; old enough to vote, or die in Vietnam or any other war my government sent me to, legal in any bar in the land.

I didn't die in Vietnam, just got a Purple Heart and some shrapnel in my spine that still aches in cold weather. It's throbbing right now in the raw December rain, as I crouch surrounded in the land of national monuments: over my shoulder Lincoln's marble Gettysburg Address; through the bare trees Washington stabbing the sky like a bayonet; a grenade toss away three grunts like me frozen in bronze, twenty years old forever.

A stark black ribbon of dead names scrolling downhill at my feet.

It's amazing how the mind works, incomprehensible almost how my first sight of the Vietnam Memorial brings back not the war, but that word MANIAC taut across a T-shirt with a loud woman inside. I never saw her or it again. In the meantime, our leaders saw the light at the end of the tunnel and realized that while eighteen is old enough to get killed for your country, you must be twenty-one to legally start doing it to yourself with alcohol.

"Hey baby," the woman cried as I left the bar. "Lighten up. Rome wasn't burned in a day."

# Sidecar

A month after the Woodstock festival I broke my ankle playing soccer. Not that I was *at* Woodstock. I'm sure a few thirteen-year-olds were there, though the pictures I'd seen in *Life* magazine were mostly of little kids and people in their twenties. People like my neighbor Mark's older brother, a.k.a. the coolest person in the universe because he went to Woodstock with his friend on a Harley with a sidecar. He had long, bushy hair and a mustache like Dennis Hopper in the *Easy Rider* movie poster. I had a crewcut like a soldier, but I knew that was about to change along with the rest of the world.

Because the world obviously *was* changing. Protesters in the streets were going to stop the war in Vietnam, and probably all war forever. Woodstock had shown that peace and love and music were all that mattered. I didn't know if I would ever smoke grass or trip on LSD, but I knew that I *could*. The new world waiting for me had no limits.

All of that stayed true, but a few things happened. Soon after returning from Woodstock, Mark's brother held me thrashing underwater in their pool till I was sure I was going to drown, then called me a faggot and laughed as I ran home bawling. A kid kicked me from behind and snapped my ankle, and I spent the whole soccer season in a cast. In December, violence and death at the Altamont concert in California made Woodstock seem like a long time ago. People said Altamont's ugliness put an end to the sixties, but the calendar said that was going to happen anyway. In a few weeks it was Christmas, and then 1970.

The world was still waiting for me, though it didn't seem quite so new. My parents gave up the battle and my crewcut expanded into unruly curls. That spring, Mark's brother got drunk, wiped out around a curve and crashed the Harley into a stone wall. After that his brain worked in slow motion and he walked with a limp. He couldn't drive a car, much less ride a motorcycle. I didn't think he was cool anymore, though I was still afraid of him and tried never to cross his path.

Jimmy Carter was president the only time I rode in a sidecar. I was at a party and mentioned my neighbor's journey to Woodstock, and somebody's boyfriend offered me a ride. I was tripping on peyote that day, so details are hazy, but there's a faded Polaroid of me in a Disco Sucks t-shirt, grinning helmet-less as a guy I just met is about to tool around the block with my nervous ass a few inches off the street.

Which is when I learned that sidecars are scary and godawful uncomfortable. We didn't crash or even come close to crashing, but I've rarely felt more vulnerable than in that little one-wheeled coffin. The coolest trip of all time was replaced by the reality that traveling hundreds of miles to Woodstock in that thing would be torture.

I was twenty-three and hadn't played soccer in years. A couple of months later the seventies were over.

# Bludgeonism

My neighbor George Wood is a pretty naïve guy. You'd have to be naïve to host a Saturday morning public-access TV show called *Wake Up with Wood*, right? No sense of irony, no clue as to how many jokers have chortled over that moniker. I doubt he even knows what "double entendre" means. He probably just likes the "w" alliteration, though chances are he doesn't know that word, either.

George asked me to be on the show this week. You might wonder who watches a lame local program at six A.M. The answer, surprisingly, is lots of people, which for me is the point. I don't feel like getting up so early, but that's a minor piece of the problem. The major piece is Candace, my fiancée.

The problem isn't that we're getting married. I want to make that perfectly clear. The wedding was her idea, but I'm definitely down with it. Candace also has a sense of humor, and would probably be tickled rather than ticked off by being called a "major piece" (not that I'm going to mention it and find out).

So what's the problem? In a word—Candace's word— "bludgeonism." It's how she describes George's lack of subtlety, which I admit is staggering. He's that way when he offers to "blow the balls off" the woodchuck eating my garden (um, probably not, George—it's a suburban neighborhood), and he's that way on his TV program--which we'd never seen before but recorded this morning to take a look. He's not exactly a Fox News type, more of a dream-world libertarian who quotes Thoreau and Thomas Jefferson, but only the parts that support what he wants to believe, and often don't even do that because he misinterprets them. The kind of citizen who hates taxes and votes to slash the municipal budget because it's "so full of fat it's about to have a coronary," but calls the town hall to complain if a pothole near his house isn't fixed right away.

Anyway, here's the rub: after I spent four years writing my first novel, and two more searching for a publisher, *On the Black* recently came out with a small press. Hand to Mouth Books did a great job but has zero money for advertising, so when George invited me on to discuss the novel, I was psyched to get some publicity.

But twenty minutes into the show, Candace shakes her head. "Don't associate your brand with that moron and his bludgeonism."

My "brand"? "How could he get political with a book about minor league baseball?"

"He'll find a way. Besides, his viewers don't read literary fiction."

"Sounds kind of snobby."

"Sounds kind of true. This nitwit says 'physical' year instead of 'fiscal.' You don't want to be associated with him and his Flat Earth Society audience. They call themselves Woodies, for god's sake."

Candace has a tremendous point, as usual. But after an initial "surge" to the 84,579th spot on the Amazon sales list, *On the Black* has dropped below one-millionth place. Six years of work, and my book is already sinking into the quicksand of obscurity.

"What do I have to lose, except maybe pride? Elvis sang 'Hound Dog' to a Basset Hound on TV and sold ten million copies."

"He said it was the most embarrassing experience of his life."

Maybe so, I almost tell her, *but he sold ten million records.* Selling even 1,000 books would be success beyond my craziest opium pipe dream.

Ten minutes on my goofy neighbor's show, or my future wife's respect? (Not that she'd hold a grudge if I *did* go on; that would be ridiculous.) It probably wouldn't lead to many sales anyway, just make me a punch line (at least in my own house). On the other hand, Wayne Gretzky said you miss 100% of the shots you don't take, and the experience might give me something quirky to write about. I'm actually kind of curious. I haven't been on TV since *The Ranger Robbie Show* when I was six years old.

"It would be awkward to turn George down now."

Candace looks like she just bit a lemon. "Jesus, Matthew, grow a pair. Want *me* to do it for you?"

At first I think she's offering to grow a pair, then realize she means break the news to George.

"No, it's my responsibility."

I'll tell him as gently as possible. I don't want to beat the poor naïve schmuck over the head with it.

# Pretty Good American

My car needed an emissions test, so I took it to the Ford dealership. In the waiting room two men sat across from each other at a table, ignoring a game show on the TV. I walked by them on my way to the coffee machine.

"You talk pretty good American," said the grandfatherly-looking guy in a MAGA cap. "Where you from?"

The other man was maybe thirty-five. He wore a New York Yankees cap.

"Ecuador," he said.

"Ecuador? This place must seem like paradise compared to Ecuador."

I stopped in mid-pour and put back the carafe. I took my half a cup to the table next to them.

The immigrant wrapped both hands around his Styrofoam cup. He stared down for a few seconds, then turned toward the patriot. "I think they are both nice," he said.

"So, do you have your green card?"

"No."

"Why not? You're illegal?"

"Citizens do not need a green card."

The American took off his MAGA cap and tapped it on the table. He leaned back in his chair, peered up at the television. "Well, that's just…that's just fine. Welcome to the greatest country on earth."

An employee poked his head in the door. "Eduardo, your vehicle's ready."

The newer American nodded and stood. He swallowed the rest of his coffee.

"Thank you, sir. I have lived here for sixteen years, but thank you." He tossed the cup in the trash and left.

I waited for the patriot to make some comment. He knew I had heard every word, and I obviously did not look like I came from Ecuador, though Sweden was a possibility. Instead, he put the cap back on his head, adjusting it just so, and began watching *Let's Make a Deal* like I wasn't even there.

# About the Author

Tom Hazuka has published the novels *The Road to the Island*, *In the City of the Disappeared* and *Last Chance for First*, as well as over seventy short stories, two books of nonfiction (both co-written with C.J. Jones), and a memoir, *If You Turn to Look Back*. He has edited or co-edited ten anthologies, including *Flash Fiction*, *Flash Fiction Funny*, *Flash Nonfiction Funny*, *Sudden Flash Youth*, *A Celestial Omnibus*, *You Have Time for This* and *Flash Nonfiction Food*. His most recent book is *Operation Panic: Cold War Stories of the Atomic Bomb*, edited with Jimmy J. Pack.

Tom is also a singer-songwriter; links to his writing and original songs can be found at <u>tomhazuka.com</u>. He taught fiction writing at Central Connecticut State University for many years.

www.ingramcontent.com/pod-product-compliance
Lightning Source LLC
Chambersburg PA
CBHW030337020726
47493CB00004B/1300